W H JOHNSON

THE MACARONI DANCERS

and other stories

DOWNSWAY BOOKS

First published in 1992
by DOWNSWAY BOOKS
P O Box 296, Polegate, East Sussex, BN26 6ZQ

Printed and bound by Antony Rowe Ltd
Chippenham, Wiltshire

British Library Cataloguing-in-Publication Data:
A catalogue record for this book is available
from the British Library

ISBN 0 9518564 0 5

The stories in this collection are set in 1939. The background owes much to South Shields where I spent the first twelve years of my life. Yet I am not specific about locations although there was an 'Imperial' cinema and there still is a ferry and a market place and the ladies, ever naked still, hang around the Town Hall. But as for the 'Sir Robert Peel', I am quite sure that such a public house never existed where, in my mind, I have placed it.

The representation of dialect has been a problem. Make it too rich and it's hard to read, impenetrable in fact for 'outsiders': water it down and the stories lose any sense of place. The greatest difficulty has been what to do with 'me' and 'us'. In these stories I have frequently used 'us' in place of 'me' as happens in Tyneside speech and sometimes I have put 'wuh' instead of the plural 'us'. For instance, 'He told me' comes out as 'He told us' which is confusing but unavoidable. If there had been more than one person involved, instead of 'He told us' I could have written 'He told wuh'. I hope it works, the way I've tackled it. I've taken advice, of course, but if I've got it wrong the fault is mine.

In conclusion, I offer my grateful thanks for their help and encouragement to my writer friends and especially those in Battle, Bexhill, Eastbourne, Hastings, Lewes and Tavistock. I also thank Mary Morton of Alfriston who has wordprocessed this and other manuscripts, often at great speed and always with great accuracy and patience.

W H Johnson
Alfriston, East Sussex
March 1992

For my mother, Jennie Johnson

WELL KEPT SECRETS

It was always easy enough to believe what Spuggy Robson told you. Most lads used to listen to what he said. He'd stand there with his head shaven, just a little bit fringe on the front, and the britchey backside of his short pants open to the sky, and you'd believe every word he said. And he had such words, words you'd never heard before, great long'uns, and him only thirteen.

"Ah know how they get that way," he was saying. He was whispering as if he had confidential information and he didn't want anybody but me to know. "Ah know how they get theirsel's fit." He stood back and folded his arms as if he was trying to keep the cold out. "Ah know how it all starts."

If only he would tell us, I thought. How did Raich Carter get his goals for Sunderland? How had Tommy Farr stood up to Joe Louis? How did Len Hutton score 364 at the Oval? And how did Johnnie Weissmuller run so fast, jump so far, and fight crocodiles with his bare hands? Would I ever be like any of them, a super fit hero?

"Course ye could be like them, man," Spuggy told us. "Ye could be like all o' them."

Could I? Really?

"If ye started soon enough. That's all it takes. Them fellers all started at about your age. That's why they're world-beaters now."

He looked us up and down very carefully.

Thirteen and he knew everything.

"It's all in the trainin'," he said. "An' Ah can tell ye what it is."

He looked over his shoulder. There wasn't a soul in sight but he still came closer and whispered in me ear.

"It's secret, like," he said. "Ah don't want ye goin' an' tellin' other lads."

I'd never dream of breathing a word. I told him that.

"Ah've got their fitness plan. All their secrets. Ah can make anybody who wants into a super fit hero."

I was on the point of asking him where he'd got his information but he told me first.

"Me dad knows this feller," he said. "No bother. Knows everythin'. Knows everybody. Top Man. Secrets of the famous."

Spuggy winked at us. I knew that he couldn't say any more about where he had heard the plan.

"Ah can't tell ye this feller's name but ye've heard of him. Ye'd be surprised to hear who it is."

He stood back for a moment, sort of weighing us up as if he wasn't sure if he should say any more but I seemed to pass the test. He took me arm.

"Basic fitness is the secret," he said. "But ye have to develop it carefully."

And Spuggy knew how to do it.

"Nowt to it," he said. "Sign up wi' me and Ah'll make ye like Raich Carter in no time."

And Len Hutton, Tommy Farr and Johnnie Weissmuller.

"Ah'll train ye. Get ye to the peak of perfection," he said. "It's not everybody Ah can offer this to but you've got natural ability. Ah can see that."

I didn't exactly sign anything but I agreed to let him be

me trainer.

"It's runnin' wi' weights that does it," he said at last. "That's what it's based on. That's the essence." He knew all about essences. He used to talk about them a lot.

"But we'll do it wi' newspapers," he said. "That's how they did it. All them fellers. They all started wi' newspapers."

"Usin' them as weights?"

"Exactly."

"Runnin' with them?"

"Aye."

"Sellin' them?"

"Aye."

But there was lots of newspaper lads and they weren't all becoming world famous.

Spuggy laughed as if I'd said something daft.

"Course not," he said. "They don't go about it the right way."

Then I said I'd seen him selling papers and he wasn't playing for Sunderland or fighting crocodiles. And he had the secret.

He just laughed.

"No," he said, shaking his head. "Ah've no interest in being famous. Ah just know how it's done."

I'd seen him often enough, selling his newspapers. He never seemed to go more than a trot. Mind, if it was dry and warm enough, unlike this particular day, he never wore boots when he was selling so the soles of his feet were like leather. And his legs were skinny, what you could make out beneath the layers and streaks of mud and general muck.

But I did want to be fit. And famous. And I'd come to the right lad.

"Right," he said. "The special regime is this. Ye come to the corner of Langtry Terrace every night at five. On the dot. Punctual. Ah'll give ye ya bag o' papers. 'Evenin' Chronicles'. Ye'll run as fast as ye can for a whole hour with the bag. That's the regime."

I told him I understood. I was looking forward to the regime bit.

"Exactly an hour. To the minute," he said. "An hour's arduous training."

Thirteen years old and he used words like 'arduous' in the way the other lads said 'table and chairs'.

Then he explained. There was twenty-five 'Evening Chronicles'. I had to sell them on the way.

"That'll reduce the weight, ye see, as ye get tired. That way ye can keep up the momentum."

I understood that as well. Even 'momentum'. He made it sound so good. I wasn't only going to get super fit. I was going to keep up the momentum as well.

And then he mentioned the bonus. Not only was he looking after me training but there was a bonus.

"Sell all the twenty-five and give us the takin's and you get tuppence bonus."

It seemed marvellous.

"Ah like the idea," Spuggy said, "'cos it makes ye into a real professional sportsman. You're gettin' paid to train, ye see?"

Paid to train.

Like Tommy and Len and Raich and Johnnie.

"And ye'll have ya own special area to run round."

"When the weather's better, will Ah have to do it in bare feet?" I asked him.

He thought not.

"Have ye got a pair o' sandshoes?"

"Aye."

He seemed to think that would do. I was relieved.

"And do Ah have to have a permit?"

"No. Ye don't need a one workin' for me," he said. "Ah've got a permit but you don't need a one. Mine covers you. It's what ye call comprehensive."

Comprehensive, mind.

But me mam and dad?

"Ah wouldn't bother tellin' them," he said. "Just say

you're comin' out trainin' wi' me."

So that's what I told them. I said I'd be running with Spuggy every night, five till six. Getting fit. Improving me muscles.

"They could do with improving," our Maureen said. "They're like spiders' kneecaps."

"Well, don't get overtired," me mam said. "If ye get tired just sit down and get your breath back."

I said I would. But I knew I'd be busy keeping up the momentum. I wouldn't be stopping to get me breath back. I'd be busy with the regime as well. And the essence, most likely.

"Anyway, who is this Spuggy?" me mam asked.

"A lad from school," I told her. "One of the big lads."

"Ah hope he's sensible," me mam said.

"If he is, that'll make one of them," our Maureen said.

Me mam was more concerned at that time with old Mrs Morris downstairs. She'd been ill for a long time and for the last few weeks me mam had been looking after her. She used to cook her meals and take her drinks of tea and do her washing and make her bed and go messages for her.

"She's got a son," me dad used to grumble. "Why can't he come over?"

"He's busy, Ah expect," me mam'd say. "He's got a very responsible job."

"His missus could come," me dad'd say.

And there wasn't any denying that. The son came rarely enough and his wife hadn't been to visit downstairs for the last twenty years as far as anybody knew. And the old woman never went to their house which was only a mile or two away. It was a fine house, by all accounts.

Anyway, me mam didn't complain. She was up and downstairs a dozen times and more every day. Never once did she say a cross word about it.

But me dad did.

Spuggy told us exactly how to shout 'Evening Chronicle'.

"Aye," he said. "Bring it out loud and long. It's good for ya lungs."

I was sure it was and as I ran, I used to shout it out every quarter of a minute or so.

"Ee-hern Corr-o-nie-a-c-ule"

He told us I never had to stop running. If somebody wanted a paper, even when I was fishing it out of the bag, even when I was scratching in me pocket for change, I had to keep jog trotting.

"Ye'll feel the benefit," he said.

And every night when I set off he used to remind us about getting back on time.

"Back here prompt, now," he used to say. "And Ah'll pay ye ya bonus if ye sell ya twenty-five papers. But ye mustn't be over time. The trainin', ye see."

When I used to get back he was very fussy about the time.

"Ah'll have to penalise ye, mind, if you're over the hour."

He used to check me time on a 'Mickey Mouse' watch, only he wouldn't call it that. 'Ingersoll', he used to call it.

The first three nights was agony. Me feet were sore and I had a blister. It was freezing cold and I kept slipping on the icy cobbles. When I got home I used to fall asleep straight after tea. In the mornings I was so stiff I could scarcely walk.

"You're overdoing it," me mam said on the Wednesday night. "Ye don't want to overdo it."

But I took no notice of her. I knew it was doing us good. Spuggy was certain I was improving by the day.

"That's it," he said. "And when you're stiff that's when you're really feelin' the benefit."

By the first Saturday night I was nearly all in. I'd run and run and run. I was grateful that Sunday was me day off.

When I met Spuggy at five on the Monday he was full of confidence. He thought I was looking even trimmer, he said.

"Hurt?" he said when I told him it was painful. "Course it hurts, man. That's what bein' a professional's like. It has to hurt. Think of Tommy Farr."

I did. I thought of Tommy Farr. I kept on thinking of him. And of the others. Nothing else but the thought of Raich Carter and that lot could have kept us going. That and Spuggy reminding us that I was just like them, another professional.

The only difference was that I was an unpaid professional. But I stuck at it. Six weeks I did it. Six weeks of frost and ice. The thing is that in six weeks I never got any bonus. I never managed once to sell twenty-five papers. Sixteen and seventeen, yes. Some eighteens. Twice I sold nineteen. No more. Never twenty-five. But I kept on trying.

"Hard lines," Spuggy used to say. "Keep at it. Don't let disappointment get ye down. Never mind, lad, you're looking very fit now. Ah'm just wonderin' how ye would compare with the young Johnnie Weissmuller. Not far off, Ah'll bet."

Me mam was with Mrs Morris when she died. She went and cleaned things up and then she called in the doctor. After that she went down to the Town Hall, to Mr Morris's office, to tell him his mother had died.

That night, when I got in from training, me dad was looking a bit fed up. He'd just come in and he was still in his work clothes.

"Ye've what?" he was saying. "They're coming here?"

"Yes," me mam said. She was looking a bit guilty as if she knew what he was going to say.

"Forty of them?" he said. "Forty bloomin' strangers?"

She pretended not to hear.

"Comin' here for the funeral 'do'?" he said.

Me mam started messing about at the sideboard.

"They can't have it downstairs," she told him. "It's a mess."

And it was. Had been for years. And me mam couldn't make it otherwise.

Then she told him she'd seen Mr Morris in his office that morning. He'd said how difficult it was to have people in his mother's house, the way things were.

Oh, they could come to our house, me mam had said. Use our place. It was only for a couple of hours or so.

"What about their place?" me dad asked her. He was speaking quietly, trying to control hisself. "They've got a grand big house."

Me mam shook her head.

"Ah don't know," she said. "It's a bit difficult for him."

She shrugged.

"And you're doin' all the food?"

"He's going to pay for it," me mam said. "Ah'm not doing it for nothing."

Me dad gave a great sigh.

"Ah should think he is," he said. "Ah should just think he is goin' to pay."

"It's just a few sandwiches and a sponge cake," me mam said. "Something like that."

She looked down at her feet as if she didn't want to talk about it any more. Me dad gave a bit of a laugh.

"Aye," he said, "and trifles and queen cakes and some spice cake. And mebbes a bit of cold tongue and some boiled ham."

He shook his head in amazement.

"And he'll pay for the food right enough, but you'll do all the preparin' and the waitin' on. And there'll be forty of them."

Me mam was looking down at her hands.

"Right," she said after a while. "That seems to be the menu. Thanks for your help."

She went out into the scullery.

Me dad went and leaned against the doorpost. He took his time, standing there, filling his pipe.

"Aye, well," he said at last, "poor old soul, ye can't have a funeral and nowt for the mourners."

Me mam came back in, brushing past him. She was smiling quietly to herself.

"By," me dad said, "you're a funny woman."

She still said nothing.

He went over to the window and looked down into the back yard for a bit. Then he turned round, looking very serious.

"Ah hope you're not bringin' the old lass's body up here, as well," he said. "She was a canny enough soul, but there is a limit."

I remember the day of Mrs Morris's funeral very well. The weather was a bit warmer than it had been but it was a dull, heavy sort of day. It was the day I decided to give up Spuggy as a trainer. I'd had enough. All I ever wanted to do when I got home was lie down. And I didn't really feel any benefit from what I was doing. Me muscles didn't seem any bigger from what I could tell. And I still hadn't been paid any bonus. After six weeks, mind.

On the way home from school, I felt quite relieved it was over. I was going to see Spuggy and tell him I was finishing straight away, no hard feelings.

Just as I reached our street I saw our Maureen ahead of us with another lass from her school. I could see she was trying to impress this lass because she was a greengrocer's daughter and paid school fees. Our Maureen was waving her arms very excitedly because there was a car at our door. It was a little Austin Seven.

"Oh," she was saying in her cut-glass voice. "I wonder who can be visiting us."

There was a little, skinny, baldy-headed feller at the

front door shaking hands with me mam.

"Must be one of mummy's friends," our Maureen was shrieking. "Perhaps he's been for afternoon tea."

She made you sick the way she showed off. She was as edgy as a raggy mat.

But he'd been for tea, all right. Him and forty others. It was Mr Morris and he was thanking me mam for what she'd done.

"Mummy's always entertaining," I heard our Maureen telling the lass.

But she got no answer.

I took the smile off both their faces.

"It was humiliating, mam, right in front of Norma," our Maureen said later when she got in the house and Mr Morris and his car had gone. "It was degrading in the extreme."

One thing about our Maureen, you could bank on it that she took advantage of her education. She never heard a fancy word at that Convent School of hers that she didn't trot out within twenty-four hours.

"Oh, take no notice of'm," me mam said.

She looked at me.

"Ye shouldn't do that in the street," she said.

All I'd done was me impersonation of Tarzan's ape. I was quite proud of that. I used to do it at school. Of course, our Maureen hadn't liked it. And obviously the greengrocer's daughter hadn't been over keen.

But me mam couldn't be bothered to say anything more. She was dead tired. She'd had a busy few weeks and she'd ended up with a 'do' for forty. She just asked our Maureen to help with the dishes.

"What about him?" our Maureen said.

But me mam took no notice. Perhaps she didn't want to overtire us before I went out with Spuggy so I didn't tell her I was going to see him to call off me training.

I changed into me black sandshoes and I was on me

way downstairs into the backyard when I heard our Maureen shouting after us. Normally I'd've ignored her but me mam had been on my side today so I thought I'd better stop in case she wanted us to do something.

Our Maureen was smirking at us from the top of the stairs.

"Here, Tarzan of the Fleas," she says. "There's a job for you."

And she held an umbrella out to us.

"Mam says you've to take this. Mr Morris left it. You've got to take it to his house."

"Tonight?" I said.

"Now," our Maureen said. "Straightaway."

Then me mam appeared at the stair top.

"Yes," she said. "He needs his umbrella. He's very important at the Town Hall."

And she told us where he lived.

Well, I'd go after I'd seen Spuggy, I told her.

I was at the end of Langtry Terrace at the usual time. Spuggy came struggling up with a huge sack of 'Chronicles'. He had nothing on his feet, sure sign the weather was a bit better. By the time he got to me, he was reaching in for me bundle of twenty-five.

"No, Spuggy," I said. I kept me hands tight round the umbrella. I was a bit worried. "Ah'm not doin' it any more."

You should've seen the look on his face.

"Ah'm packin' it in," I told him.

He frowned, looking very serious.

"Ye cannot do that, man. Ye cannot pack it in," he said. "Not like that."

I moved from one foot to the other. I gripped the umbrella tighter.

"Ye cannot pack it in right in the middle of ya trainin'."

The trouble was I didn't know how to answer that.

"D'ye think Len Hutton would've scored all them runs if he'd packed his papers in?"

Still I didn't answer.

He talked about Tommy Farr. He'd stuck by his papers and so had Raich Carter. They'd both found it hard but they went on with it. Look where it got them. Johnnie Weissmuller had once wanted to pack in but he didn't.

"There'd've been no crocodiles for Johnnie Weissmuller if he'd packed in sellin' his papers."

But even so, Spuggy couldn't persuade us. He frowned a bit more, then changed his tack.

"Ye cannot just gan up to the gaffer and tell'm you're jackin' it in."

"Aye, well," I said and stopped. I started to open and shut the umbrella.

"Ye don't think ya dad can gan up to the gaffer and say he's off."

He put his hand to his chin and stroked it very slowly, all the time staring hard at us.

"Where d'ye think ye'd be if he did that? And ya mam? And your Maureen?"

I didn't know so I didn't say anything.

"It's not the way to do business," he said.

He was standing on one leg, trying to get a small piece of gravel out of his bare foot.

"Business isn't done like that, lad. Ye have obligations."

He'd lost us. More long words. I didn't know what he meant. I was stroking the umbrella. It gave us a bit of comfort.

"Business is economics. It's based on trust," Spuggy was saying.

I was still lost.

"You're my employee," he said. "Ah pay ye."

I understood that.

I managed to tell him that he'd never paid us anything, not yet. More than six weeks and I'd never had a penny bonus from him. I'd sold a lot of papers. Never quite twenty a night but still a lot.

"No," he said. "That's 'cos you're still in trainin'. Ye've not learned the business yet. Ye've taken advantage of me knowledge but ye've still got a long way to go."

It was true, really. I'd had his help and encouragement.

"You're a source of grave disappointment to me, ye know." He shook his head.

He made us feel really guilty so I turned away. I was blushing for shame.

"Ah'm sorry," I said and I began walking away. Why couldn't I stick it out like Johnnie Weissmuller?

"Hey," he shouted. "Come here."

I heard him come after us.

As I went to face him, he got hold of the umbrella by the handle and I just managed to hold on to the end of it.

"Gizzit here," I said.

"No," he said. He gripped it tighter.

"Come on."

"No."

I gave it a tug but he held on.

"When ye do two more nights," he said, "ye can have it back."

"No," I shouted. "Ah want it now. It's not mine."

"Not till Ah can replace ye," he said and he gritted his teeth.

"It's a feller's. Ah've got to take it to his house now," I said.

I gave another tug, then suddenly I shrugged me shoulders. I smiled at him. He relaxed and when he was off guard, I gave another tug.

He was older than me but he wasn't all that strong. Newspapers hadn't done all that much for him, I remember thinking. Anyway I gave it another almighty tug and got it from him. All but the handle. And I ran.

When I got to the house it was nearly six and it was quite dark already.

It was a big place, just like me dad said.

Me stomach was turning over. I'd spent the last half-hour working out how I'd explain about the umbrella handle. I thought I might say somebody'd bumped into us and I'd dropped it. But it didn't sound very good.

I went up the path and rang the bell.

Nothing happened.

I gave another ring.

More silence.

I began to hope there was no-one in. I could leave the umbrella there. When they came back, when they found it broken, I could say it was all right when I left it, if anybody asked.

Then a light came on. I could see it through the fanlight. There was a rattle of bolts and locks. Finally, the door opened.

I couldn't make out what the woman looked like, but the way she looked down at us made us think she was a bit on the sour side. And her voice certainly was.

"Can't you read?" she said.

Before I could answer she was darting in with another question.

"Did you not see the notice on the gate?"

I wasn't sure at first but then I remembered seeing a little white plaque.

'No Trespassers,' it said. 'No Hawkers. No Circulars.'

I knew I wasn't a Trespasser. I wasn't sure but I didn't think I was a Hawker or a Circular either.

"You should've come round to the side," the woman said. "What d'you want?"

I held the umbrella out towards her, trying to keep the handle part away from her.

"Well?" she said. "What's this?"

She was staring down at the umbrella. I wasn't sure if she recognised it.

"Me mam sent it," I told her. The words were hard to get out, me mouth was that dry.

"Your mam?"

"Yes," I said. "He left it this afternoon."

"Who did? What are you talking about?" She was a very irritable woman.

"The feller," I said. "Mr Morris. He left it. When he was at our house."

I told her where I lived.

When she didn't answer, I thought I'd better make things clearer.

"After the funeral," I told her.

Even though with the light behind her, I couldn't make out her features, I could see there was some kind of change in her. She suddenly seemed to get smaller. And then, she took a step back as if she'd been punched in the chest. She put her hand out and held onto the door knob. At first I wondered if she'd seen the umbrella handle was missing and it had upset her.

"Funeral?" she said.

Then it dawned on us that I must've come to the wrong house. I was trying to work out what to say to her when I saw a movement behind her at the end of the passage.

"Who's that?"

It was a man's voice.

He came up the passage. A little, skinny feller. Baldy headed. I was at the right house, all right.

"Who's that?" he asked again.

The woman turned to look at him.

"Who is it?" she said. Her voice went really high. "Who is it? You've got a nerve asking who it is."

As she was speaking he seemed to shrivel up just as she had done before.

"What is it, dear?" he asked her. But his voice was very faint. It could scarcely creep down the passage.

"A funeral," she said. "Your mother's."

It was ages before he spoke again. He just stood at the

end of the passage saying nothing till suddenly he straightened up. Then he yelled out loud as anything.

"Yes. My mother's funeral today."

And he stopped again.

And then he said in a very quiet voice, "And you've never gone to see her or asked her here in twenty years."

He put his hand to his eyes and it looked as if he was going to cry.

"Never in twenty years. D'you expect .... ?"

Then the woman shut the door in me face. Never even said thank you for the umbrella. But I left it outside the door.

On the way home I met Willie Scott. You'd never forget Willie. His face was always covered with dabs of purple for his impetigo. He looked exhausted. He was nearly in tears.

"Ah'm packin' this up," he said, throwing his sack of newspapers down on the pavement. "Spuggy's had it. Four weeks of this an' me impytigo's no better."

And he'd never had any bonus either. Some seventeens. A couple of eighteens. Twenty-two one night. If Spuggy'd only let him do over the hour he'd sell twenty-five, he was sure.

"He says it'll flare up if Ah gan on more than an hour," Willie told us. "But at least Ah'd get a bonus."

There was three or four other lads as well, he said. One of them had bow legs and another one of them used to have fits. They weren't too satisfied with Spuggy's remedy either. Newspaper selling wasn't making a ha'porth of difference, they were saying.

Nobody as far as I knew ever sent any thank you to me mam for what she'd done for old Mrs Morris. I expect her son had said something when he last saw me mam at our house but he never wrote. And we never heard anything about the umbrella.

When me dad said, “Ye wouldn’t expect owt from them,” she just shrugged her shoulders.

When he told her she shouldn’t waste her time on folk like that, she just smiled.

“Ah didn’t think it was a waste of time,” she said. “She was a good neighbour to us.”

Me dad raised his eyes to the ceiling.

“She thought the world of her son,” me mam said. “Never saw anything wrong with him.”

“No,” me dad said. “She didn’t. But she should’ve done.”

But me mam shook her head.

“No,” she told him. “She shouldn’t’ve seen anything wrong with him ... that’s not the way ... no, she shouldn’t ... never .....”

Anyway, I gave up running seriously. I sprained me ankle soon after so that really put the tin hat on it. By the time I was fit again, I was doing lifting exercises with the flat irons. I thought it was really doing us good. So I just kept that up. Even me dad admitted, the muscles in me arms were coming up a treat.

CUCKOO

No good trying to explain.

"Nine o'clock here," me mam says. "Ah've been worried sick."

She's said that four or five times already.

"Ah don't care about the blessed searchlight."

She's said that as well.

"As far as Ah'm concerned they can just forget their searchlight. Ah'm not interested. You shouldn't be on the streets at this time of night. A lad your age."

And on and on about the time and how it's a wonder I haven't got me death of cold.

"Ye can get to bed," she says. "Straightaway."

And later she comes in with a cup of something or other.

"Here, drink this," she says. "Ye must've been frozen out there all that time."

But I wasn't.

If me dad had been in, if he hadn't been on late turn, he would've listened. He would've been interested in the searchlight. I was sure he would because loads of people were. There was crowds looking at it, where they'd put it on the waste ground, all of them staring at the beam, following the length of it up into the skies. And there was little flashing specks in it, like little darting fish, dancing in the light. It gave off a groaning sort of hum and even though it was so low and quiet a sound, you could hear it above the shouts and talk of the people.

The soldiers kept swinging it round and turning it off and on and pointing it at different corners of the sky. And you thought, well, if a war breaks out, if that Hitler starts owt, he's got a shock coming when he finds out about this searchlight. That'll put the kybosh on him.

And looking at it, at the great, fat, silver beam, you forgot about the time and the frost and the sharp wind. You never gave them a thought.

Well, I never gave them a thought.

But the next day, when I saw me dad before he went to work, me mam had already got at him.

"You're not going out any night for the next week," he said.

That was that. I didn't argue. Especially when me dad had me mam behind him.

I stayed in the next six nights when I could've been out doing nobody any harm. I desperately wanted to get back to see the searchlight even if it was only for a few minutes. Sometimes from the window I could see it chasing across the sky but that wasn't the same as being there, where the light started.

On the seventh night, I thought I'd try me luck. After all, even prisoners get time off for good behaviour. Me dad had just come in from work and while he was waiting for me mam to get his dinner he was standing warming hisself by the fire.

"Can Ah go out tonight?" I asked him suddenly while me mam was in the scullery.

Before he had a chance to answer, me mam came in.

"No," she said without looking at either of us. "Ye can just do as you're told."

She wasn't pleased about something. But it wasn't me.

It was me dad. She'd been on to him about me Auntie Louie's birthday present. Me dad had had one of his good ideas. They'd been arguing about it for weeks.

"D'ye think your Louie wants something like that?" she asked him. "She's a young lass. She doesn't want that sort of thing."

Me mam was very protective about me Auntie Louie because she was so young.

"Ye'd think ye'd know your own sister's tastes," she said.

Me dad sort of blew out his cheeks and sighed.

"He's a skilled craftsman, ye know," he said. "He's really good. He's very clever with his hands."

"Poddy Grace is not a skilled craftsman," me mam told him very firmly. "He has never been a skilled craftsman. He works in an ironmonger's."

Me dad had to agree with her on that.

"But he's a clever feller with his hands."

Me mam gave him one of her looks.

"Ye've never seen anything he's done. Ye scarcely know him."

Me dad was twisting his pipe in his hands. I knew he was wishing now that he'd never asked this Poddy Grace to make whatever he was making for me Auntie Louie.

"Ah've heard about his work. He's got a reputation," me dad said.

"He's got a reputation all right," me mam said. "Everybody knows about his reputation except you."

"Aye, well. He'll be round with it and that's what we're givin' our Louie," he said. "So that's it."

Me mam went out into the scullery.

"So that's not it," she shouted through. "If it's not up to a decent standard, she'll get something else."

They said no more about it and I can't say I was sorry. Even our Maureen had lost patience and she didn't join in either.

When we sat down to eat, me mam looked at me.

"You asked to go out tonight."

Me spirits lifted.

"Well, ye can't. One reason is that Ah promised to call over at Mrs Allen's. She's not been over clever."

Mrs Allen was always ailing. And of course me mam had been roped in - or more likely volunteered - to keep an eye on her. Always doing good, me mam. Well, I thought, for other people anyway.

"And Ah've got a snooker match at the Club," me dad said.

He was keen on his snooker and this was a handicap tie. He couldn't miss that.

"And I've got Guides," our Maureen pipes up.

I'd forgotten that. She was doing her advanced test for boiling an egg or something of that kind.

"And Poddy might call round," me dad said. He looked at me mam. "It's not definite but he'll be along one of these nights soon."

Me mam kept her eyes on her plate. She didn't look up when she spoke.

"He promised it for three weeks ago," she said. "What makes ye think he'll have it ready before another three weeks?"

Me dad just gave a laugh but he was very ill at ease. He didn't say anything.

"That's the thing with these religious people," me mam said. "Always saying they'll do things."

"Well, he's a decent enough feller," me dad said.

"Ah'm sure he is," me mam said. "But he's not good at making things on time. And from what Ah hear he's not good at making things of any kind."

Me dad sat back in his chair.

"Wait an' see," he said. "Ye'll be pleasantly surprised."

"Ah'm sure," me mam said, almost to herself.

Seven nights in the house on the trot exhausts any interest you might have in the wallpaper or the lights or the carpet and curtains or the table and chairs. And then, to be left on your own, to be deserted. I was really fed up, desperate you might say. There was nowt on the wireless. Just a talk on birds. Mebbes later it would be all right. I liked 'Monday Night at Eight'. That would be all right if I didn't go mad beforehand.

Then something struck us. It was me birthday in a few weeks. I'd be eleven. Sometimes they bought me presents early. Like for Christmas they used to get them at the summer sales. And for me birthday they sometimes got them in the January sales. Me mam always used to hide me presents under the bed or on top of the wardrobe in her and me dad's bedroom. They were the usual places but sometimes they found other places because they were suspicious of us. Good rights to be.

Anyway, I had a bit of a look round. Nothing on the wardrobe top. Nothing inside. Nothing under the bed. Nothing in the cupboard under the stairs. Nothing in any drawers anywhere in the house. There'd be something for us. Surely.

The sideboard drawers had table cloths in them. Some of them were still wrapped up in their paper from the shop. There was a big box with knives, forks and spoons that we never used. Then, in the side cupboard, I found some bottles. Me mam and dad never drank in the house, except at New Year. They didn't take the bottles out from one year's end to the other.

There was a bottle of ginger wine there. I loved the stuff. I used to have it every Christmas and New Year. So I gave meself an excuse. I went down to the coal house in the yard and filled the bucket slowly. It was freezing down there. Then when I came back up and I'd put some more coals on the fire, I poured meself a cupful of ginger wine. I'd really earned it. I needed to warm meself up.

By, it was lovely. It went down a treat. At least it made up for being kept in. I pulled up the chair close to the fire and out of the draught and I supped me ginger wine. I was thinking I might have another, it was so nice. After all, nobody'd notice. It'd likely be next year before anybody even looked at the bottles.

I was just about to fill me cup again when there was a knock at the front door. For a moment I wondered if I should put the bottle back in the sideboard but then there was another knock, even louder, so I dashed downstairs.

When I opened the door there was a feller standing there with his shoulders up to his ears and his hands deep in his overcoat pockets.

"Good evenin'," he said. "The Lord be with ye."

I tried to get a good look at the feller but it was dark and I'd forgotten to switch the light on at the top of the stairs.

"Is ya dad in?" he said.

Poor feller, it was so cold his teeth were chattering. Then I saw a little lad with him, standing back, all crouched up as well. Only he was worse off because he was just wearing short trousers.

"No," I said, "he's not in."

"Oh," says the feller, "'The good man is not at home. He is gone on a long journey.' So says the Good Book."

He was standing there stamping his feet as he spoke. So was the little lad.

"No, he's not gone far," I said and for a second or two he stopped his stamping. "He's playin' snooker."

Then he said, "Is ya mam in then?"

I told him she wasn't.

By now, I'd had a look at the lad and then, even though it was dark, I recognised him.

"Hello, Eric," I said.

Before Eric answered, the feller said, "Oh, so you're acquainted with Eric."

I said I was.

"Ye know this lad?" he says turning to Eric.

"Gans to school wirrus," I heard Eric mutter. Eric

always muttered. Nobody'd ever heard him speak louder than in a mutter. He wasn't in my class. He was a year younger. But I knew that much about him. He was well known for his muttering.

"Eric," the feller said, and never taking his eyes off him. "Now, listen." He paused a bit. Then he spoke very slowly. "He goes to school with us." He shook his head, as if he disapproved very strongly of Eric. "'Goes' not 'gans', man. I keep tellin' ye. And it's not 'wirrus'. It's 'with us' or 'with wuh'."

The feller looked back at me.

"Ah've come to see ya dad, really," he said. "Ah've been doin' a little job o' work for'm."

He lifted a leather bag he was carrying up onto his knee. He opened the zip.

"Ah'd better tell ye," he said while he was taking a cardboard box out of the bag. "Ah'm Mr Grace."

So I understood now. It was Eric's dad.

"Have ye heard of us?"

I told him I had. I'd heard me mam and me dad talking about him only tonight.

"Ya dad's been expectin' us to bring it along."

I remembered what me mam used to say about never keeping people on the step.

"D'ye want to come in?" I asked Mr Grace.

"It is a bit cold out here," he said. "Ah'll come up and show ye what Ah've done."

I led them upstairs to the kitchen. The fire was roaring away.

"By lad," Eric's dad said, looking round the room, "it's better up here than outside." He put his hand on his chest and looked up at the corner of the ceiling. "'The winds blew and beat upon that house, and it fell not: for it was founded on a rock'," he said. He smiled down at Eric. "That's right, isn't it, son?"

Eric said something but I couldn't hear what it was. He just stood hunched up, his little face white and pinched and the insides of his legs chapped and raw with cold.

"Ah don't know when they'll be back," I said to Mr Grace.

He sort of nodded as if he was trying to look very wise. He was the funniest looking feller. What I noticed about him was his shine. I'd never thought before of anybody being shiny but Poddy Grace shone like owt. His face was dead white but every part of it, forehead, cheeks, nose, chin, absolutely shone as if he'd washed and washed hisself and then dried and dried hisself and finished hisself off with a chammy leather. And when he took his cap off the whole of his baldy head shone. And even his blue suit had a shine to it. It had been worn and worn and ironed and ironed so that you'd think it was made of some kind of metal. And right across his stomach there was a gold chain hanging from one waistcoat pocket to another, and he had an Albert hanging from it. The whole lot shone like Christmas lights. And just to glance at his boots nearly blinded you.

"D'ye want a cup o' tea?" I said.

Poddy Grace's face lit up.

"Very kind," he said, "very kind. 'God loveth a cheerful giver', eh, Eric?"

Eric nodded. He looked as if he needed a hot drink. He was still huddled up and his teeth were chattering.

"It'll not take long," I said.

I thought me mam would be proud of us. "Always offer a visitor a cup of tea," she used to say. "That's manners."

"What ye got in that cup?" Mr Grace asked us just as I was taking the kettle off the hob to put in the centre of the fire. "Ye been havin' yaself a drink, eh?"

"Ginger wine," I told him.

"Ginger wine?" he smiled. "Why, if it's all the same to you, Ah'll have that. Champion stuff for a night like this."

I was quite pleased. I'd rather give him the wine than make tea. And he could take the blame if anybody did notice the level in the bottle had gone down. So I poured him a cupful. Then I poured one for Eric and another one for meself.

"Warms ye up, this does," says Mr Grace. "Doesn't it, Eric? Warms ye up, this stuff, eh?"

"Aye," Eric muttered.

"Can't hear ye, Eric, when ye mutter like that," his dad said. "No good if ye cannot be heard."

He put his lips tight together as if he was going to say some more but then he changed his mind. He tapped the cardboard box that he'd put on the table.

"That's what ya dad's waitin' for," he said. "D'ye want to see it?"

Of course I did.

So he opened the box.

Would you believe it? It was a little wooden house.

Under the red gable was a pair of blue shutters. They were closed. Under that was a white balcony and it had little red flowers painted on it. Then there was a yellow door. The whole thing was very bright and just like the places you see in pictures of Switzerland.

"What d'ye think o' that, then?" he asked us. "What d'ye think, then?"

I didn't know what to think. I was just surprised at me dad asking somebody to make a little doll's house. And I wondered if me Auntie Louie wasn't a bit old for it. Then I noticed the faintest of numbers in a circle, painted almost the same brown as the walls of the little house.

"Very nice," I said.

"Aye," Mr Grace said, and he put his head on one side, "and our Lord was a carpenter an' all."

"I really like it," I told him. "It's really nice."

Mr Grace smiled as if I'd congratulated him for building the Tyne Bridge or something. He was going to say something else when he stopped, looked us up and down, glanced at the ceiling a bit thoughtfully, and then said, "Ye haven't a sup o' port wine to go in here, Ah suppose? Just to take the edge off it." He smiled encouragingly. "Ah find ginger wine just a bit sharp. In fact, it reproves on us, makes us bowk."

Ginger wine, port wine. It was all the same to me.

"'Use a little wine for thy stomach's sake'," Eric's dad was saying, "'and thine often infirmities.'"

Mebbes next time I'd try the port wine meself instead of the ginger. I looked inside the cupboard. There was a bottle of port wine, nearly full.

"Champion, son," Mr Grace said when I poured some into his cup.

"Not for Eric," he said, putting his hand over the lad's cup. "And Ah don't think you'd like it either," he said to me as if he'd been reading me mind. He raised his cup to his mouth and tried it. He seemed to like it.

"'Eat thy bread with joy'," he said, "'and drink thy wine with a merry heart - for God now accepteth thy works.'"

He took another sip and ran his tongue round his lips.

"Look at this," he said. He took a key out of his pocket and held it up in front of me face. You'd think I'd never seen a key before. But then he was off, winding up the house at the back. In no time at all, it was ticking away like mad.

"Now," he said, sticking his hand into his waistcoat pocket, "just to complete the job ......" And he took out a little piece of paper. He opened it.

"These is the things, eh?"

It was the pointers.

"Ah'll put them on now so ye can see the job bein' completed." He screwed the clock pointers into place between the balcony and the door. "There now. All complete. Ye've seen the cuminilation of me labours."

He put his head down into his hands as if he was praying. After a bit he looked up.

"Now, lad," he said. "Watch this." He put the hands on one minute to eight o'clock. "Watch and listen."

Right on time, right on the hour, out comes the

cuckoo. He had a red and white body, green eyes and a bright yellow beak. And he didn't just come out. He went back in. Eight times. And each time he came out he cuckoo'd.

"Did you make that?" I asked Mr Grace.

"Ah did," he said and he puffed his chest out. "All by meself." He took his cup from the table and took a drink. Then he put the cup down and looked at us a bit sorrowfully. "Sinner that Ah am," he said, "Ah neglected to mention the help of the Lord." He lifted his cup up again and swallowed what was left.

"Ah wonder .... ?" he said, holding the cup out to us. "Don't bother about the ginger, son," he told us. "Ah'll leave that for you and Eric. Or there'll not be enough for you."

So I topped up Eric's and me own.

A minute later, the cuckoo was out again, singing his nine o'clock song and shortly after that he did the ten o'clock shift. Then, the eleven. 'Cuckoo', he went, sweet as a nut. Then round and round we went, me and Mr Grace and Eric, stopping every hour. And every time, on the hour, out popped the cuckoo, regular as owt, regular as clockwork.

"So," Mr Grace said, "ye know how it works and ye can tell ya dad."

I could. I was looking forward to that.

I filled Mr Grace's cup three or four more times and he sank back very contentedly in his chair. And every time he knocked it back and held his cup out for another fill-up.

" 'Be not drunk with wine wherein is excess'," he told us, "'but be filled with the Spirit.' "

I didn't really know what he was getting at so I just said, "Right-o, Mr Grace."

"Have ye seen the light, son?" he asked us suddenly.

I told him I had.

"Wonderful," he says.

It was, I agreed. I didn't tell him of course that I'd

been kept in seven nights because of it.

"Our Eric, here," he said, "saw the light two years ago."

That was a bit much, I thought. They only put it up ten days ago.

"It was at Morecambe," he told us. "At the Annual Missions Conference."

Well, he might've seen it at Morecambe, wherever that was, but we hadn't had a light here until ten days ago. No doubt about that.

"He's goin' to be a preacher."

Mr Grace leaned over and touched Eric on the head very gently.

" 'Great was the company of preachers,' " he said very quietly, still with his hand on his son's head, " 'Kings with armies did flee.' "

Eric a preacher? I didn't think he'd be chasing off kings and armies. I thought preachers had to talk a lot. Eric never said much and when he did you couldn't always hear him.

"He's studyin' hard for it," his dad said. "Aren't ye, Eric? Aren't ye studyin' hard for to be a preacher?"

"Aye," Eric said in his usual low voice.

" 'Yes', Eric," his dad said. " 'Yes' is what what we say, isn't it? We don't say 'Aye'. Do we? Not when we're goin' to be preachers."

I think Eric said, "Yes".

"He's preachin' at the Convention next year at Scarborough." Mr Grace gave a little nod and smile as if he'd just heard the news. "The boy preacher. They'll be queuin' up to hear'm. Won't they? Queuin' up, eh, son?"

Eric didn't seem as excited about it as his dad.

" 'And a little child shall lead them,' " his dad said.

Eric didn't look as if he would ever lead anybody anywhere.

"Just another half cup, son," Mr Grace said, nodding at the bottle. "Just afore we gan ... go."

He seemed to like the port wine well enough. And his face was a bit pinker than when he came in.

"He's been doin' elocution, ye know," he said. "Ye can't do the Lord's work unless ye talk properly." He nodded at his son, sitting quietly inspecting his hands. "Can't preach the Word of the Lord if ye can't speak well."

Mr Grace went quiet for a bit, smiling to hisself. He reached over and tapped Eric on the arm.

"Gan on, son. Tell'm what ye've been doin' in elocution."

Eric whispered something.

"Speak up, man," his dad said. "Nobody can hear ye talkin' like that. Ye'll not have to talk like that at Scarborough. They'll never hear ye past the first row."

Mr Grace looked angry and he was swaying a bit in his chair.

"No good payin' for elocution lessons and you takin' no advantage," he said. He turned towards me. "The cuckoo clocks, ye know. That's what pays for Eric's lessons."

Eric cleared his throat but when he finally spoke his voice wasn't much louder than before.

"Ah go to lessons. To learn to talk. So Ah can preach the Lord's Word."

" 'Watch and pray,' " his dad said pointing at him. " 'The flesh is weak.' "

"They're learnin' us to speak differently."

Eric's dad took another swig from his cup. He winked at us.

"Gan on, Eric," he said. "Let's have some of the words they've learnt ye."

Eric cleared his throat again.

"Orinoco," he says.

"Hear how he says it?" his dad says loudly and very proudly.

I hadn't really noticed anything.

"Say it again for'm, Eric."

"Orinoco," the lad says again.

"Hear that?" says Mr Grace.

I said I'd heard it right enough.

"Give'm some ordinary words, Eric," his dad said. "Mebbes he doesn't know about Orinoco."

Eric nodded and licked his lips and made a couple of false starts. Then it came out.

"May Aye have sam co-oold peese pooding and ay rasher of bay-eecon?"

"Hear that?" his dad yells, smashing his hand hard down onto his thigh. "Hear that? 'May Ah have some cold pease puddin' and a rasher of bacon?' " Mr Grace shook his head as if he was amazed at what he'd heard hisself say. "Ah never had much education meself, but our Eric's gettin' it." He put his hand on me shoulder. "He's goin' to be a great preacher."

Suddenly I saw the tears in his eyes and his lips begin to quiver.

"A great preacher," he said again. " 'Ye have not chosen me but Ah have chosen you.' "

He rubbed his eyes with the back of his hand.

"He'll not have works canteens or fish 'n' chip shops for his dinner. Nothing like that. He'll be in an office and he'll go out to cafes for his dinner."

Mr Grace shook his head in wonder as if he could already see Eric having his dinner in a cafe.

"He'll be so grand and famous he'll not want to talk to his mam and me." He sighed. "And we'll be so proud of'm."

Over in his chair Eric was squeezing his hands together as if he couldn't quite believe he was going to be as great as his dad said.

"Ye'll have to excuse us a minute," Mr Grace said. He wiped a great fat tear from his cheek as he stood up. "Ah'll have to go to the lav."

He went out through the scullery and down the stairs and into the back yard. He seemed to have a bit of difficulty on the stairs. I heard him at the bottom and then there was silence. Then he shouted up to us.

"Is there a candle in the lav?"

I told him there was. If he was like me he'd want it just to keep his hands warm while he was sitting there.

Eric hadn't moved. In fact he'd scarcely moved at all since he came in.

We sat in silence for what seemed ages. I think Eric was embarrassed at his dad for crying. I was just as embarrassed for Eric with his dad making him talk like that.

"It's a river in South America," he said suddenly. Just that sentence, nothing more. I didn't know at the time what he was on about and I didn't ask. It was only later when I realised he was talking about the Orinoco. I never thought that was a very useful piece of information but I suppose saying 'Orinoco' over and over again must make anybody a better speaker.

When he came back upstairs Mr Grace was whiter than when he first came in. What bit of hair he had was soaked and his forehead was spattered with little dots of sweat. He was breathing heavily as if the back stairs had been over much for him. Anyway, in he came.

"D'ye want to go?" he said to Eric. "To the lav?"

Eric shook his head.

"Right then," Mr Grace said, buttoning his overcoat. "Ah think we'll be off."

Eric stood up and fastened his jacket. His dad suddenly stopped moving. He mumbled a few words to hisself. Then he put his hands on both our shoulders, Eric's and mine.

" 'The night is far spent, the day is at hand,' " he said. " 'Let us therefore cast off the works of darkness and let us put on the armour of light.' "

I wondered if he was describing his suit. That was like an armour of light, I thought.

"Don't forget," he said. "If ye need the Lord's consolation, come to the Mission. We'll always be there if ye need wuh."

He belched softly.

"Pardon me," he said.

We all went down the front stairs into the street. It was bitter.

"Ah hope ya dad likes the clock," he said.

I said I thought he would.

"And thank ye for the hospitality." He patted us on the head. "We'll away then. 'Ah will return into my house from where Ah came out.' "

Eric said "Thank you," very quietly.

"The Lord be with ye," Mr Grace said.

He turned and put his arm round Eric's shoulder and they walked together a bit unsteadily down the street till I lost sight of them between the street lamps.

When I'd put the bottles and cups away, I had another look at the clock. It looked really smart. I thought me Auntie Louie'd be really pleased with it. I got the cuckoo to come out again and he did the whole trip from one till twelve. And every time he came out fresh and sharp, on command. Well, he did until he tried twelve for the fourth time. He just couldn't manage the shutters. They only just opened a tiny bit. I could see the beak for a second or two, glistening through the crack. Then it was hidden again. I thought of him stuck behind there, straining to get out, trying to knock the shutters open with his shoulder so that he could do a bit more singing. I put the pointers back to eleven and he made a bit more effort but he wasn't successful. Mebbes he was sulking in there. Being stubborn mebbes, sick of overwork. I had to laugh at the thought.

He couldn't or wouldn't come out at ten. Nor at nine.

I tried ten again and eleven and twelve. But he couldn't budge the shutters.

And worse, the clock stopped. I gave it a shove but that did no good. I was getting a bit worried. I wound it up again and it gave a half dozen ticks and then nothing more. This was getting serious. I wondered if I should take the back off, but it was nailed and glued. I was near tears. I began to sweat. I didn't know what to do. At about nine o'clock - real time not cuckoo time - I heard the front door rattle. They were back. It was me dad with our Maureen. He'd finished his game and he'd called for Maureen at Guides. He looked really pleased with hisself and I could tell without asking that the snooker had gone well.

"You're what?" me dad said. He was surprised. "Goin' to bed already? What's up with you?"

It was about me usual bedtime but I didn't volunteer as a rule.

"He's been up to something, dad," our Maureen said, full of Girl Guide importance.

"Oh, Mr Grace has been here," I said to me dad just as I was going out of the room. "He's brought ye a clock." I'd put it on the sideboard.

"Oh, good." Me dad smiled. "Have ye seen it?"

"Yes," I said. "He let us see it."

Me dad was quite excited. He reached over and picked the box up. "D'ye want to see it, Maureen?"

I was just out of the door when he called us back.

"Where's the key?"

It was on the mantlepiece.

"Wait a minute, man," me dad said. "Let's have a look together."

He held the clock out towards Maureen.

"Bit bright, isn't it?" she said.

"Well made, though," me dad said. "Look at it." He turned it round in his hands.

Maureen took the clock from him. She scratched off a bit of flaking paint from the shutter. She found a small splinter of wood hanging off the side of the gable.

"Skilled craftsman, did you say?"

"Why, he's not a full time carpenter or owt," me dad said. "It's more a hobby."

"Hm," our Maureen said. She'd picked that up from

me mam.

And then, me mam walked in. She took the clock out of our Maureen's hands.

"So that's it," she said after she'd inspected it. "That's one of Poddy Grace's masterpieces, is it?"

"Aye," me dad said, not very sure of hisself.

"And Ah'm to take that to your Louie, eh?" Me mam gave him a very hard look. "And what's this?"

On the sideboard was a white card that Mr Grace had left behind. Me mam picked it up and studied it. Then she read what it said out loud.

"'And the sea gave up the dead which were in it; and death and hell delivered up the dead which were in them: and they were judged every man according to their works.'"

We all stood around silent for a bit. Then me dad spoke.

"Well, be reasonable. When it's hung up on the wall and goin', it'll be worth seein'. It'll look real nice. Cheers the place up, a cuckoo clock."

So he wound it up.

And we waited.

And waited.

Poddy Grace's name was mud in our house. I never told them how he was doing it all for Eric to be a great preacher. I didn't think they'd see it that way.

Even though it was Saturday night, they were still testing the searchlight. Me dad and me were there from about seven till gone nine. It was a marvellous sight and even though it was still bitter cold, there was lots of people there.

Me dad had been quite keen to bring us over to see the light. He was glad to get out of the house because me mam kept on about Poddy Grace and his cuckoo clock.

On the way home, we stopped a minute for me dad to fill his pipe. We stood under a street lamp while he did it.

"Those are really good clocks, ye know. Poddy Grace's quite good! whatever your mam says. An amateur but ye know .... "

I agreed. The clock looked good. Neither of us mentioned the flakes of paint or the splinters of wood on the side.

"Ah don't know why it won't go," he said. "Mebbes the clockwork's not up to it. Foreign, Ah expect. Poddy's not responsible for the clockwork."

He puffed on his pipe till he got it going. Then we walked on. We didn't talk for a bit but when we got near the house, he put his hand on me shoulder and we stopped again.

"Ah shouldn't tell ye this," he said. "Ah was going to get ye one of them for your birthday. Ah thought it would look well in your room."

"It would, dad."

He sighed.

But if the bloomin' cuckoos won't come out," he said, "there's no point."

Just before he opened the door he said, "Ah'll have to get your Auntie Louie somethin' else, Ah expect."

Well, me mam did. She bought her a pair of sheer silk stockings with seams. Me Auntie Louie was pleased as owt with them but I did wonder if she'd have been even more pleased with the cuckoo clock.

They got me a pair of football stockings for me birthday. I was really pleased with them. But just sometimes when I looked at the blank space on the bedroom wall, I wondered if a cuckoo clock, even if it didn't go, would have been even better.

TRIP OUT

Me dad always sneered at the tea leaves and when me mam said, "Ah'm going to have an unexpected trip out," he just kept reading his 'Chronicle'. So me mam said it again.

"Ah'm going to have an unexpected trip out."

Me dad cleared his throat. We waited for a reply, but then he just sniffed and turned the pages very noisily.

"Don't ye want to hear?" me mam said. She was smiling. She was bursting to tell him.

"Not particularly," me dad said.

"Come here then," she said to me. She took us by the arm. We went into the scullery. "We're not going to let him know. Old Misery," she said, making sure he could hear.

I heard him give a kind of snigger and I knew everything was all right. At first I thought they were rowing which they didn't often do. But they weren't. He was just showing her what he thought about the tea leaves.

"Ah'm going on an unexpected trip out," me mam told us.

"Ah know that, mam," I said. "Ah've heard you say it twice already. Where ye goin'?"

I'd picked up a bit of me dad's impatience. If he could be snappy, so could I, over this matter of the tea leaves.

"Where'm Ah going?" she looked puzzled for a moment but then her face cleared. "Why, don't be daft. They don't tell you that. Ye don't get details."

I don't think she really believed in any of it. She just liked to go along to Mrs Baty's whenever they had The Divorced Woman in to read the cups. Me mam used to go along there two or three times a year and when she came back she was always full of it, what The Divorced Woman had seen in the tea leaves.

"Could be anywhere," she said.

"Could be nowhere," me dad growled from his chair.

"You're not supposed to be listening," she shouted, looking round the door at him.

"That lad's more to the point," me dad said. "Ask him what he's been up to."

Not that he cared if I got into little bits of lad's bother. In fact, I think he quite enjoyed it. As long as I didn't tell lies or hurt anybody, he was always good-natured about me little bits of daftness.

But me mam's face changed. She always worried if I upset the neighbours or anything like that. If I did anything that made people think we weren't respectable, she'd get really worked up. "We might not have a lot of money," she used to say, "but we are a respectable family."

Anyway this time all the excitement brought on by the tea-leaves disappeared when she heard what me dad had said.

"Well? What you been up to?" she asked me.

It wasn't much really. Not a lot. Just a window. Not ours. Three doors along. And a football.

"Ah've told ye not to play football down there."

But if I didn't play football down there I'd be cutting meself off from the world. Everybody played down there. In the street. At this time of the year. We hadn't time to go up to the field, the nights were so short.

"We're all clubbin' up," I told her.

"Oh," she said. "Right. Well as ye've no money to speak of, Ah suppose ye'll want a loan."

"Aye, mam. A shillin'."

There was no hesitation. Out she came with it almost before I'd finished speaking.

"Right. Ye can have it."

She was good to me, me mam.

"But this time ye can pay it back as soon as possible."

"Right." Now I didn't feel so sure. I thought something was brewing.

"No pictures this week."

I couldn't believe me ears. No pictures this week? It was me life's blood. I depended on the pictures. And this week at the 'Imperial' they were showing the last reel of 'The Lone Ranger'. I thought I knew which one of them it was but I'd like to be sure. There'd been six at the start. Then one by one they'd been killed. Now there was only two. And Tonto.

"Time you learnt a bit of responsibility," she said. Two or three minutes ago she'd been wanting to tell us about the tea leaves. She'd dragged us into the scullery. Great joke really between her and me dad. And me. But now, I was all that was bad. Irresponsible. Really she didn't like us playing in the street. I suppose that's what it was.

She was as good as her word. The week passed. Everybody else had been to the pictures except me. I could put up with that. But on Saturday they showed the serial. And everybody I knew, all the lads, would be there. They'd be there to cheer the credits and then the action. They'd already cheered the shooting down of the fourth ranger as they had the first three. They'd cheered the escape of the fifth and sixth ones with Tonto. They'd cheered all that. But when it came to the last shoot-out you'd be able to hear a pin drop. And then, after that, well, the cheering would go on for minutes and the ushers would come down with their torches and wave them about and threaten to chuck you out if you didn't behave and make less of that noise. But they never did anything really because all the bairns were yelling their heads off and standing up and punching each other. Smashing. Anyway, the thought that I wouldn't see the real Lone Ranger unmask hisself was a terrible blow. I felt really down. And nobody in our house seemed to understand. And our Maureen was very skitty. Seemed to be enjoying it. Of course, with her at that Convent School, she was supposed to be above all that sort of thing.

"Childish," she said in a voice that would cut cloth. "Cowboys and indians."

That Convent School had a lot to answer for.

On the Saturday morning, I was just going down Bell Street when somebody shouted at us.

"Want a game, lad?"

It was Skinny Jobling from my class. He was standing at the door of his dad's shop.

"Want a game?" he asked again. "Haway in the yard."

He had a football in his hand. I never refused the chance of a game of football so we went through the front shop and through the workshop. There was two fellers working there, sawing and hammering coffins. Skinny's dad was into funerals in a big way. He was noted for his posh coffins and his grand horse-drawn hearses. We went into the yard.

"Haway, Skinny," I said, "three goals in" and I stood just where a double door into the workshop made a good goal. Skinny took the ball down the yard. But all he did was mess around, dribbling it past imaginary defenders and whispering to hisself something like, "Now, Jobling has the ball for Sunderland. He's a marvel."

Well, if he was Sunderland, I was Newcastle.

I was getting impatient because he was very slow in shooting at goal. He was just playing by hisself, doing all sorts of fancy tricks. It was easy enough when there was no opposition.

"Wonderful, Jobling," I heard him say. "What a difference this young player has made for England."

England now, eh?

"Haway, man, Skinny," I shouted. "Giz a look in."

I didn't want to leave what I'd worked out was my area so I stayed more or less in the middle of the goal while he jigged around in the area between the coal house and the outside lav.

"Haway, man, Skinny," I said and I suddenly took three or four strides down towards him.

He looked up. He was waving his hips and making little darts left and right and he was holding his fingers out delicately. I don't know who he modelled hisself on but he didn't look all that impressive to me. Anyway, he starts running at us with the ball at his feet. I scrambled back to goal and crouched ready for him. Headlines were already racing through me mind - "Young Goalkeeper saves the Magpies", "Brilliance in Goal by unknown lad". I narrowed me eyes, poising meself ready to dive wherever he placed it. He was coming up fast, still whispering to hisself. He drew back his right foot.

That's when he fell.

It was just the smallest chock of wood from the workshop. A tiny piece. But Skinny Jobling, international footballer, idol of Roker Park, managed to put his foot on it. And over he went.

"Well tackled," I shouted. I didn't half laugh.

But he didn't get up. He lay in a heap, groaning.

"Ah'm injured," he moaned when I went up to him.

"Haway, man. Get up," I told him.

"Ah cannot, man. Ah'm hurt."

He brought his leg from under him. His ankle was already blown up.

"Ah'm in trouble," he said.

"Aye," I said. "But ye won't have to go to school."

"No. But Ah'm on thissafter."

"On thissafter?"

"Aye. Ah'm on."

"On what?"

He looked at us painfully.

"Me da'll be furious," he said ignoring me question.

"What for?"

Again he ignored the question. Instead he said, "It's all your fault, lad."

"My fault?"

"Aye."

"What'd Ah do?"

"Gettin' impatient. Hurryin' us up."

"Why, man," I said, "ye were a bit slow."

Then his dad came.

"What's up with you?" he asked.

"Ah've hurt mesel'."

He showed his dad his ankle. Mr Jobling looked down at it.

"But you're on this afternoon," he said as if he couldn't believe what he was seeing.

"Ah know," Skinny said, bursting into tears.

"What'm Ah goin' to do?" his dad said. He looked at Skinny as if he wanted to bray him. "Ah need ye."

But Skinny had no answer.

His dad turned his back, gave him a very long and very angry look and went back into the workshop.

"Can ye get me mam for us?" Skinny asked.

So I went into the house and Mrs Jobling came out and we got Skinny back inside. I waited while she stuck his foot in a bowl of cold water.

Then Skinny's dad came in. He was in no better temper.

"What'm Ah goin' to do?" he asked his wife. "Ah need'm."

"Well," she said. "There's no possibility of ......"

She suddenly turned to me.

"What about him?"

All in all, and looking back, it was quite interesting. I'd never done it before and I've never done it since. Well, you don't see that sort of thing these days.

Luckily, I was about the same size as Skinny so the black suit fitted. And I was in long trousers so I felt quite grown-up. And it wasn't all that difficult. I just followed Mr Jobling. I don't know if he was still in a temper but it didn't show from the back. He was a fine looking feller really and he walked in front. I just had to go about the same pace.

"Don't go lookin' round," he said. "Just keep your eyes on me. When Ah stop, you stop."

So there was Mr Jobling, me, a horse-drawn hearse with a bairn's coffin in it, and a parade of about fifty mourners behind.

I did as I was told. I kept me eyes straight ahead. In any case, I knew that if I didn't, if I moved me head, the topper would fall off. That was the only part of the outfit that was a shade small. So, as I'd been told, I kept me eyes straight ahead on Mr Jobling's back.

I didn't even move me head when I heard a man's voice say, "Ye bugger, that's wor lad, isn't it?"

When I swivelled me eyes, I saw me dad was standing on the pavement's edge, his cap in his hand. His mouth had fallen open and he was half turned to me mam. Our Maureen's face was bright scarlet.

But then, I turned my eyes back on Mr Jobling.

I did what I was told and kept me eyes straight ahead till we got to the cemetery.

I didn't know how me mam and dad would take it. But when I got in, me mam came over to me and kissed us on the forehead. Over in his chair, me dad said something but I couldn't make out what it was. Perhaps he was saying something about the football results in his paper.

"Would ye like to go to the pictures, tonight, pet?" me

mam asked.

Would I? The Lone Ranger was going to unmask hisself.

"Ah'll pay for ye," me dad muttered. "Ye can both go. Ah was goin' to anyway."

"Great, dad. But Ah'll pay for me mam."

'Cos I was flush.

I had half a crown. Not bad for an afternoon's work.

"Oh," me mam shouted. "This is me unexpected trip out." She looked at me dad. "Ye see. Doesn't pay ye to scoff at the tea leaves."

OARY VAW

The trouble with Noble Patterson was that I never really liked him. Worse, me mam seemed to think he was marvellous. Probably because his dad worked in the Water Board office and went to work in a suit.

"Such a nice mannered lad," me mam used to say and our Maureen would chip in with some remark like, "And not silly like some", as if all the lads I went out with were stone-mad.

But whatever they said, they couldn't persuade me to like him a great lot even though sometimes I went out with him, when he called for us which he did every so often.

"Here's Noble," me mam says one Saturday afternoon, looking out of the window as he's coming up the street. "Isn't he smart?"

"Isn't he just?" our Maureen says and she opens the door.

Noble's in a nearly new jersey and his stockings are pulled up round his knees with never a wrinkle in them. And he's spotless.

"Puts you to shame." Me mam doesn't say it but I can read her mind from the way she looks across at us, as if she's comparing me with him.

"Ah'm just wonderin' if ye'd like to come down town," Noble says. He's got this very polite, well-mannered look on his face.

And I'm doing nothing. I've spent me pocket money. I've no big ideas on how to pass the day.

"Aye, right-o," I tell him.

I get me coat on and me muffler and me mam comes over fussing and fastening buttons and doing things with me collar.

"And where d'ye fancy going?" she says. She's attending to me but the question's for Noble.

"Just round the market an' that," he says. "Just have a look round."

And they're thinking what a sensible lad he is and what a credit he is to his mam and dad. You can tell it by their smiles, me mam's and our Maureen's. And Noble smiles back at them.

That's why I never really took to Noble. Always creeping up to folk, trying to please them, get in their good books. And the other lads never really took to him. It wasn't just me.

Me mam's in such a good temper she gives us a tanner.

"There now," she says. "Don't spend it all at once."

And she means it.

Then I see our Maureen. She's giving us a very peculiar look. I don't like it when she's got that face on.

"Come back 'n' have your tea, Noble," me mam says.

"Oh, aye, lovely, Ah will," Noble says, very enthusiastic, which only goes to show that he was the sort of lad who said what he didn't mean.

He smiles at me mam and our Maureen in turn.

"Oary vaw," he says.

I'm looking puzzled and he turns to me, very superior.

"That's what they say in France when they say goodbye," he says.

Show off.

We're just going down the back stairs. Noble's in

front. “Good job ye’ve got that tanner,” he says to us. “Ah’m stony-broke.”

I was wondering if that was why he’d come round on the off chance, when the door behind opened.

“Hey.”

It’s our Maureen whispering down the stairs.

“Hey.”

I didn’t want to stop. Noble turned but I gave him a dig in the back. I could’ve said, “Don’t take any notice of her,” but I didn’t. I thought me push said enough.

“Hey.”

Now she’s run down the stairs after us and into the back yard.

“Just a minute,” she says. She runs across and puts her hand on the sneck before I can open the door into the back lane.

Nice behaviour for a Convent School girl, I think to meself.

“What d’ye want?” I say. I’m fed up with her, the way she goes on, pretending to be what she’s not. “We’re goin’ out.”

“I know you are,” she says with that superior look on her face. “But not before you pay your dues.”

Me dues? What’s she talking about?

“You know,” she says. “No good looking all innocent. You know well enough.”

And I do. Only it’s not convenient. Not just now.

“Look out,” I tell her. “Get out the way.”

I put me hand up to get her away from the door but she’s a big strong girl and two years older than me. She plays lacrosse.

“Go on,” she says and I have to jump back quickly before she clouts us round the ear. Then she sticks her finger in me chest.

“You can just pay up now,” she says. “You’ve owed me sixpence for the last six weeks and I’m not letting you get away with it.”

She’s on about that again.

"He's owed me sixpence for the last six weeks," she repeats for Noble's benefit. He's standing there like Toss Willie and he smiles sympathetically and shakes his head, because he's trying to stay in her good books. Then he remembers he's with me so he gives me a smile as well.

"Oh" is all he thinks of to say without upsetting either of us.

"So come on," she says, stabbing us again with her finger.

"Ah'll let ye have it next week," I tell her but I know it's no good.

"You said that last week!"

"Well?"

"And the week before."

"Ye'll have it next week," I say. "Honest."

But she's giving us no quarter. She's looking more like me mam when she's telling me dad how she feels about things.

"If you don't hand it over now I'm going back up and I'll tell mam."

Noble's moving from foot to foot as if he wishes he could get away. Our Maureen decides to keep his attention.

"I lent him sixpence for a present for mam's birthday."

She had. And I'd bought a lovely bunch of cloth flowers, all reds and yellows and greens. Me mam was that pleased with it. She'd put it in her hat straightaway and she'd worn it there ever since. It gave us real pleasure to see her wearing it. It looked so nice, the way it used to bounce up and down, all bright and colourful on the side of her hat as she walked along.

"He said he'd give it back the next week," our Maureen was going on again at Noble. "I'm still waiting."

She turned to me.

"If you don't hand over that sixpence mam gave you, I'm going straight back upstairs and I'm going to tell her that you didn't buy her anything for her birthday."

No matter what I said, she wasn't having any.

"Ah need it for me tram fare," I told her.

"You'll have to walk then," she said. "Do you good." She looked at Noble. "And don't you go lending him money," she said. He didn't tell her he hadn't any.

"No," he said. "Ah won't."

When I paid up she came away from the door. We walked out into the lane. We'd only gone a few yards and she called after us.

"Mam doesn't like it anyway," she shouted with a nasty look on her facc. "I don't know why she wears it when she hates it so much."

I was going to answer back but I couldn't think quickly enough. And it would've been a waste of time anyway because she'd already slammed the door.

We had all that walk down to the market. We were worn out nearly by the time we got there. Noble kept on and on about how good he thought me mam and our Maureen were till I felt like shutting him up. And then it started to drizzle so that I was thoroughly miserable.

We had a bit of a walk round the market but there wasn't much to look at if you weren't interested in second-hand clothes, brass fenders and sideboard ornaments. I was just on the point of saying to Noble we should go back when this lad came up to us.

"Wotcheor, Noble," he says.

Noble's face lit up.

"D'ye know Cecil Hubbuck?" he asks us.

Only by sight because he was two or three years older than me. But I'd seen him often enough.

He was a lad you couldn't miss, he was so big. And even if he hadn't been you'd never forget him because his clothes were always either too big and he was growing into them or they were too small and he was growing out of them. Everything he wore was ancient and paper thin. Cecil's trouble was that he was the middle one of seven brothers and just at the unfortunate in-between age. He was either wearing a suit with long trousers too short or one with short trousers too long. Today he had a well-patched green jacket and a pair of navy shorts, let down to his knees.

So you remembered Cecil by the variety of his clothes. And also because he had a powerful reputation for being a very dishonest member of a very dishonest family.

I was a bit worried because I'd heard all about them but it didn't seem to matter to Noble. As usual he was out to please. So he gave Cecil a broad smile as if he was never so delighted to see anybody in his life.

That was enough for Cecil. He was a cheerful enough lad so he told us a couple of really good jokes. We laughed at these and nudged each other.

"That's a good 'un," Noble says to Cecil, all smiles.

"Where yez off to now then?" Cecil says.

Of course Noble's puffing hisself out because he's so pleased a big lad's making a fuss of him, even if it is Cecil.

"Oh, just lookin' round," he says and he waves his arms about the market as if we'd eyed up all the things we were planning to buy and all the things we weren't.

"D'yez want a tab?" Cecil says suddenly and he fishes a packet of five Wood's out of his breast pocket. "Gan on," he says. "Plenty more where them come from."

Noble gives a fishy smile.

"Aye, ta," he says and he takes one of the Woodbines. He's putting it in his breast pocket and he notices Cecil eyeing him.

"Are ye not goin' to have it now?" Cecil asks, looking as if he thinks Noble's pulling a fast one.

"Oh, aye, Cecil," says Noble and his smile's quickly disappearing. "Ah was just holdin' back a minute."

"What about you then?" Cecil says to me. "Are ye goin' to have a one?"

I say something about me asthma.

"Asthma?" Cecil says as if he hasn't heard of it before. "Can't ye breathe like?"

I shake me head.

"Ah'll die if Ah smoke," I tell him. "Smokin's not good for us."

Noble looks as if he was going to say he didn't know I had asthma but then Cecil's got a box of Swans out and he's holding a lighted match under Noble's nose.

"Gan on," he says and Noble sucks away.

Then Cecil lights his own.

"It's a great life," he says, taking the smoke back right down to his toes. "Great life," he says again, and smoke shoots out of his nostrils.

"Aye," says Noble but he doesn't look convinced. He starts coughing instead.

Cecil stands back, takes another drag, looks sharply at Noble.

"Them're a happ'ny each, ye know," he says.

I see Noble's eyes close. Either he's wondering where he's going to get the money from or he's asking hisself what Cecil'll do if he doesn't pay. He seems to remember hearing that Cecil's not just dishonest. He's also a bit rough sometimes when a lad lets him down.

Noble's gone pale, dead white. Suddenly he staggers. He's sweating.

"Are ye not well?" Cecil asks him.

"Ah'm all right," Noble says, but you can hardly hear a word he says. He staggers a bit more. "Ah think there's summat wrong wi' this tab."

Cecil looks hurt. I wonder if he's drugged the tab the way they do in the pictures sometimes but I didn't think even Cecil Hubbuck would do that. Well, he wouldn't know how to.

"Nowt wrong wi' them," Cecil says. "Them's first-class Wood's."

"Ah feel rotten, but," Noble says. "Ah'm cold as owt."

All across his brow were great beads of sweat.

It crossed me mind that I hadn't seen him smoke

before. Just as well he didn't say he had asthma before I did.

"Ye'll be all right soon," Cecil says. "Giz ya tab."

Noble doesn't offer any resistance when Cecil takes the tab out of his hand. He begins to smoke both the tabs at once.

Noble sits in one of the shop doorways and puts his head in his hands.

"By lad, Ah feel awful," he says and you can scarcely hear him, his voice is that weak.

So me and Cecil think he'd better just sit there for a bit. We leave him and go for a stroll round the market. It's no better than it was a quarter of an hour before so I begin to think about going home.

When we get back Noble's standing up, still white as a sheet, but he's not staggering about any more. He's just hunched up, like a little old feller.

"Ah'm cold," he says, and his teeth's chattering.

"Haway, then," Cecil says, all smiles. "Let wuh go and have a drink. Ah'll get wuh all an Oxo."

He takes us over to one of the market stalls and has a quiet word with a fat old woman sitting there. She's got everything on this stall: clothes, little ornaments, toys of every kind. You couldn't tell what kind of stall it was. It had so many different sorts of things. In no time, we're lashing into great steaming mugs of Oxo and she's given us a pie to share as a bonus.

"For nowt?" Noble says. He's feeling a bit better now and he can think about things other than his health.

"For nowt," Cecil answers him. "That's how we are in wor family. The Oxo's on us. And the pie."

But he didn't say exactly who the fat old woman was or if she really was a relation. I wondered if he wasn't in some way saying we were really members of his family now, like blood brothers, only sealing the bond with Oxo, meat pie and tabs.

"Ye feelin' better?" Cecil says to Noble, and he takes his arm."

"Aye," says Noble. "Not so bad after the drink."

And he did look better.

"Ah've got a real good idea," Cecil tells us. He's got a bit of a sparkle in his eye and he's grinning away. "Haway, this way."

Time was getting on but we didn't like to refuse him. After all, he'd given out tabs and he'd laid on the Oxo and the pie. You couldn't ignore real kindness.

"Have ye ever been down to Richards'?" he says.

Richards'? I was never out. I'd spent hours in there. The toy shop down from the market. What a place. If you believed in miracles, that's where they happened. If you believed in fairyland, that's where it was. If you believed in Father Christmas, that's where he lived. They had everything. Boxes of lead soldiers, huge layouts of unbreakable soldiers. There was guardsmen and highlanders; there was bandsmen and grenadiers. Some of them marched upright and you could move the arm they held the rifle in. Some of them lay down, firing at imaginary targets. There was bagpipers, drummers, fifers, buglers. And there was not just soldiers and marines. You'd see stagecoaches with the drivers holding the reins in one hand and a whip in the other. There was cowboys turning round in the saddle to fire at mounted redskins. There was toys of every description. There was everything you could imagine. It was Wonderland and we were in it.

"Looka' that," Noble whispered.

"Aye," I said.

"Eee," Cecil said, breathing wonder.

All the usual stock of magic and marvel, enough to make you goggle-eyed.

And then on a little circular display counter, a Sunderland Flying Boat. You never saw anything as graceful, never saw anything as beautiful. You'd have thought it was going to take off from where it stood and fly out through the door. You could imagine it had a real engine and believe there was real people inside, ready to start it up. It was silver and for the first time in me life I thought and used the word 'elegant'. You'd have expected it to attract people for miles around just to stare and marvel at it. Perhaps they hadn't heard about it. But it was so magical you felt you wanted to shout out loud and say to everybody, "Hey, stop what you're doing. Come 'n' have a look at this." And you felt that they'd be grateful to you for pointing it out to them, that they'd thank you for showing them something they might've missed.

"Aye," says Noble, under the spell. "But looka' that. Just look at it, man."

He had his eye on a model of Malcolm Campbell's 'Bluebird'.

And there's no doubt, it was a smasher. And we stared at it a bit.

Then Cecil comes up from behind and put his arms round our shoulders.

"All right, lads," he says. "What yez waitin' for?"

We looked at him a bit surprised and we followed his glance down to his half-open palm. There's a red indian warrior lying there with his tomahawk raised.

"Gan on," he says. "What yez waitin' for?"

I'd never felt so ashamed in me life.

Cecil was walking up the street large as life, getting hold of us both round the shoulders and smacking both of us on the back. And Noble was all grins and nods as if he was having the time of his life. I was hanging back when I could. I'd never felt so rotten.

I'm looking in a shop that sells artificial legs and bed pans and wishing I was back home, wishing I'd never left the house this afternoon, wishing I'd never seen Noble and certainly not Cecil who'd come back now to the shop window. He catches us by the arm.

"Come on," he says and drags us up to where Noble's standing at the edge of the pavement, not looking at all like the sickly lad of twenty minutes ago.

"Easy, man," says Cecil, laughing in both our faces. He lowers his voice. "See how easy it is?"

He pulls us both into the doorway of a jeweller's shop.

"Dinky Toys this week," he laughs. "It'll be them things next year."

He winks towards the jeweller's window and inside, all the rings, the watches, the necklaces, seem to wink back as if they are in on the plan.

"Next Saturday, we'll try something different." Cecil says, very matter of fact. "All right?"

I look at Noble. He's got the same face he had when me mam invited him to tea. I'm waiting for him to say, "Oh, aye, lovely," just as he had to her.

"Right," Cecil says, all cheerful. "Let's gan an' see me Auntie Madge again."

He gets hold of both of us by an arm and leads us across the market place.

"Me Auntie Madge'll pay yez for them," Cecil says. "Ye'll get a good price from her."

Auntie Madge is serving a customer, but she spots us fifty yards away. You can see she's grinning at us as if she's pleased at what she sees. Oxo and pies pay dividends in her mind.

"Hallo, Auntie Madge," Cecil shouts out at the top of his voice. He waves his arms and does a little dance. "Gan on," he says. "Give her a shout."

"Hallo, Auntie Madge," Noble shouts, not quite so loud as Cecil, although he's got some enthusiasm in his voice.

And I do me best.

"Hallo, Auntie Madge."

It's not really a shout. More like a whimper.

"Get them out then," Cecil orders when we get up to the stall. He's got his red indian warrior in his hand.

I see Noble searching in his jacket. He brings out his 'Bluebird'.

I put me hand in me pocket.

"There's our Maureen," I say suddenly. I point down the row of stalls. "She's just there now," I tell them. "She'll be shoppin' for me mam. Ah've got to see her. About the tanner she took off us."

And I take off.

"Hey," Cecil shouts after us.

"Hey," Noble shouts.

Mebbes Auntie Madge shouted as well but I didn't wait to hear.

"Given it to 'er?" Cecil said when I got back.

"Ah had to," I told him. I turned to Noble. "Ye know what she's like."

He did. He told Cecil exactly what she was like.

"But did she give ye owt for it?" Cecil asked. He looked at Noble. "Me Auntie Madge gave you a good price, didn't she?" he asked him.

"Aye," Noble said. "A real good price."

"She gave'm tuppence," Cecil said.

"Aye," Noble said. "She gave us tuppence."

"What your lass give you?" Cecil asked.

They were astonished.

"Fourpence?" they said. "She's goin' to give ye fourpence for it?"

"When Ah get home," I told them. "She's goin' to give us the money then. She didn't have any on her."

But fourpence. They were amazed.

"It was only ninepence new," Cecil said. He sounded really hurt. "It's not new any more. It's second-hand." He looked at Auntie Madge. "It's not worth fourpence now, is it?"

His Auntie Madge didn't say anything but she didn't look pleased. She just went on arranging the things on the stall. When I looked at it closely there seemed to be an awful lot of Dinky Toys.

"Ah didn't think your Maureen would've taken it," Noble said. He sounded a bit disappointed. "Ah mean, knowin' how you got it."

"She's daft about this lad at the Grammar School," I told him. "She'll do owt for him. He collects Dinky Toys."

On the way back, Noble was very subdued.

"Where ye goin'?" I asked him when we got to my doorway and he went walking past. "Me mam's goin' to give ye ya tea."

"No," he said. "Doesn't matter. Ah'd better just go on."

"Is it about thissafter?" I asked him.

He didn't answer for a bit. Then he nodded.

"Aye."

I didn't know how to put it. I was ashamed of meself. I didn't know what answer I wanted from him but I asked him.

"Are ye ashamed of yourself?"

"Aye, a bit," he said and he couldn't look us in the eye.

"Are ye goin' with Cecil next week?"

He seemed to be weighing it up. In the end he said, "No. I don't like that sort of thing."

I was pleased to hear him say that.

"Ah didn't either," I told him.

I was beginning to feel a bit more friendly towards him.

"So will ye come in for ya tea now?" I said.

He waited again. Then he said he wouldn't.

"What for not?" I asked him. "Ye've always come before."

And I thought, aye, he'd come and I hadn't wanted him then.

In the end he told us.

"It was bad enough pinchin' thissafter," he said. "But the worst part's your Maureen. Ah never thought she'd take stolen stuff off ye. Ah never thought she was like that."

I couldn't talk him out of it. He wouldn't come in.

He went off not looking too pleased with life.

Oary vaw, I thought. And good riddance.

When I went in, me mam asked where Noble was. I told her he'd had to go home.

"He's a sensible lad," me mam said.

"I expect you led him into something daft," our Maureen said.

"Ye should've gone down with them," me dad said. He was laughing. "You'd've kept them on the straight and narrow."

Our Maureen sniffed.

"I don't shop in town on Saturday afternoons," she said, very hoity-toity.

"Ah suppose only the riff-raff does that," me dad said, pulling on his pipe and smiling at her.

"Make what you will of it," she says. "Anyway, I had my homework to complete."

I suppose I should've explained it to Noble but I couldn't ever bring meself to do so. Ever after that he was very off-hand with our Maureen and he never came to tea again.

Yes, I should've explained it. But I was so ashamed at letting them down in Richards'. I couldn't tell him, couldn't tell anybody, what I'd done. I mean, I'd picked it up, the Flying Boat. I'd held it. Shown it to them. I'd even put it in me pocket.

And then, when they'd seen me do that, before we ever left the shop, I put it back in its place on the display table where it belonged, ready to fly away under its own steam.

But I couldn't tell them that. Not any of them.

I was too ashamed.

ONWARD CHRISTIAN SOLDIERS

"We're goin' to the Spanish City for wor Outin'."

When Jimmy Charlton told us that I could've strangled him. The Spanish City: the greatest, most wonderful place I'd ever been to.

And Jimmy Charlton was going.

Why him? Why not me?

'Cos he was a Baptist.

"It'll be great, lad," he was saying. "Have ye ever been?"

"Aye," I said. But that was no consolation. I'd been twice as a matter of fact but it didn't look as if I'd ever get there again. At least nobody in our house was likely to take us. Me mam and our Maureen didn't like it. I mean, what sort of people didn't like the Spanish City?

"There's roundabouts there, isn't there?" Jimmy asked.

"Aye," I told him. "And swings and dodg'ems and shuggy boats. There's everythin' there."

You'd never forget the Spanish City if you'd been there. There was that roaring sound you get at fairgrounds and music and lights flashing off and on and fellers announcing attractions and people enjoying theirselves. And there was side-shows and throwing hoops onto vases and rolling pennies and rifle ranges. There was rock as well with the name right through. And when you came out the whole blooming world was jostling and joking in the streets of Whitley Bay.

It was so marvellous I could never forget it and I was so envious of Jimmy Charlton that I could scarcely bear to tell him about it.

"Ye should come with us, man," Jimmy said.

Daft thing to say.

How could I go to the Spanish City with them? I wasn't a Baptist. I didn't go to their Sunday School. Anyway, I was going up the river by boat to Ryton. With the Methodists. I'd been looking forward to that until Jimmy told us where his lot was going. I'd already got seven picture stamps on me Attendance Card. I just had to make sure I went to Sunday School the next eight weeks because you had to have fifteen stamps. They were very strict about that in the Methodists.

"Fifteen?" Jimmy said. "Ye only need six with us."

Six?

If I joined the Baptists I could get six weeks in .... but then I wouldn't get to Ryton on the boat.

Then, walking home, everything fell into place. It all seemed so simple. I thought up a really good plan. It'd only cost us six pence altogether at a penny a week. And I knew the lad who'd leap at a penny a week.

"He says he's marching with the Baptists this Good Friday," me mam said when me dad came in for his tea.

"Is he now?" me dad said. He looked at us a bit closely. "Since when've you been a Baptist?"

It was a bit difficult to explain really. Even I thought it would sound a bit daft but I said it all the same.

"Since this mornin'."

Me dad stuck his bottom lip out and thought a bit.

"Bit sudden, eh?" he said at last.

"I don't imagine he's thought it out very logically," our Maureen said. She was in the Debating Society at the Convent School so that's the way she used to talk.

"That's enough," me mam told her. "He's probably got his reasons.

I had but I wasn't sharing them.

"What's set ye on that then?" me dad asked.

"Dunno," I told him. "Just feel like it."

"Oh well," me mam said. "Ah know lots of people in the Baptists. Ye'll come to no harm there."

She and me dad didn't really mind where me and our Maureen went to Sunday School. As long as we went. Not that me mam or dad ever went to church or chapel. I think we were supposed to go and say a prayer like 'Sorry, but me mam and dad's not here but they're thinking of Ye'.

And the Marching on Good Friday would be no different with the Baptists. It was always the same. After you'd had your Hot Cross Bun with your breakfast, you went to chapel. After a lot of palaver, they got you lined up behind the banners and drums and bugles and fifes of the Boys' Brigade or the Scouts or the Salvation Army Band. Then you'd march down to the Park. It was like going to war. All the great banners, purple and blue and green and yellow, fluttered in the wind. All the bairns stuck their chests out and put their best foot forward and not a one of them was ever in step with anybody else. The lads always had their best clothes on and the girls had satin and lacy dresses and straw hats. And there was one thing you could rely on. It would be cold enough to freeze your lugs off.

"Look at the bairns," you'd hear folk say as you marched past. "Aren't they smart?" And you were part of an army and everybody was out, lining the streets, watching you. You'd catch sight of your mam and dad on the edge of the pavement and you wouldn't even dare look at them. You were so full of pride you thought you'd burst if they caught your eye.

When you got to the park you stood in a great circle round the bandstand and there'd be hymns and prayers. Then back you'd march to your chapel. One more hymn and then you lined up and they gave everybody an orange and a new penny.

It was always like that. Always had been. It was like that the year when I marched with the Baptists.

And the most important thing was that the Superintendent made a note of me name.

"Glad to see ye here, son," he said. "Comin' regular, Ah hope."

I told him I was.

"Oh good. Ye'll be comin' on the Outin' then."

"Yes," I said. "Ah'll be there."

The rest of them were in the house before me. Our Maureen had got a blister with the Methodists and was making her usual fuss.

"Here's the Baptist," she said, sneering at us.

"Very nice this morning," me mam said. "Ah thought ye were all very smart."

Out Maureen sniffed and went on rubbing her heel.

"Who was the lad with ye?" me dad asked.

"Jimmy Charlton."

"No, no. Not him. Ah know him. The other one."

"Oh," I said. "Just a lad from school."

"Aye, but, who is he?"

"His name's McCracken," I said.

"Oh," me mam said. "Does he always go to the Baptists?"

I wondered how I should answer. Eventually I thought it would be simplest to tell the truth.

"No, he hasn't been before."

After a bit me dad said, "Are ye finished with the Methodists then?"

"No," I told him. "Ah'll be goin' back next week."

"You're fickle," me mam said.

"Stupid, you mean," was the best that our Maureen could offer.

The next three Monday mornings McCracken came for his penny.

"Let's see ya Card first," I said to him every time. He'd take his Attendance Card out and I'd check he had a new stamp in it. Then I'd give him his penny.

It was working out really well. I was clocking up attendances with the Methodists meself and it was pretty sure I'd get to Ryton. But the Baptists had me name as well. I had three attendances recorded there already. Spanish City, here I come.

On the fourth Monday, McCracken didn't come and seek us out. I looked for him in the school yard but I never saw him. I didn't see him later in the day either. But he was at school because I asked somebody in his class.

Just before we started in the afternoon, I found him in the lavs.

"Ah've been lookin' for you," I said. I was very annoyed with him. "What's up?"

"Nowt," he said.

"There is," I told him. "Summat's up. Ye've been hidin' from us."

He looked really shifty, moving from one foot to the other and staring at the ground.

"There's nowt the matter, man," he said. He opened his great wide eyes and stared at us. "Only ......"

"Well?"

"Why, man, Ah like it there with the Baptists. It's great."

I found that hard to swallow.

"What's great about it?"

"Why, the singin' and the talks the feller gives ye."

"The feller?" I said. "He's not a feller. He's the

Superintendent. Ah've met'm only once but even Ah know who he is."

I must've sounded just like our Maureen.

McCracken said nothing for a bit, just went on staring at his boots. Then he seemed to pluck up courage.

"Ah'm sorry," he said and he went bright red. "Ah'm goin' to have to let ye down."

So that was it.

"Let us down? What for?"

He shuffled about, sticking his hands in his pockets and then taking them out.

"Why, it's like this," he said. "Ah've decided to gan on the Outin'. Wi' the Baptists."

To the Spanish City?

How could he?

It wasn't in his name, the Attendance Card.

How could he go? He'd be an imposter.

"Aye," he admitted that, as if he could see the sense of what I'd said, "but Ah'm an imposter anyway, using your name every Sunday."

And that was true.

"Anyway," he said. "Here's ya threepence back."

I took the money.

"Give us the Card as well," I said. "Haway, man, giz a chance."

He felt so guilty he handed it over.

"Ah'll tell the feller Ah've lost me Card," McCracken said. "He'll give us another."

I wasn't interested.

"Mebbes we can sit together on the bus," he said. "If ye can manage somethin', like."

I didn't answer him.

What I had to do was replace McCracken.

It wasn't easy to find a lad who'd go to the Baptists for the next three weeks. Not for a penny a week. There wasn't all that number of McCrackens about. It was short notice for anybody. I hadn't a lot of choice. But I found somebody.

The next three Mondays I checked the Card, paid me penny. Now I had six attendances, a full Card. The Spanish City was just a few days off. Me heart pounded at the thought of it. I couldn't sleep at nights. Saturday, I kept thinking; come on, Saturday.

"You're in trouble," our Maureen said when I got in from school on the Wednesday. She was in the kitchen and she'd already started her homework. She pretended to be concentrating but she couldn't help smiling and giving us little looks out of the corner of her eye.

"What's up," I asked her.

"Go and find out," she said and she made a great show of colouring in a map.

Me mam looked too serious for my liking. And me dad was looking a bit thoughtful.

"There's been a feller here from the Baptists," he said.

I started to tell him something about Newcastle United but he wasn't interested.

"It was the Superintendent," he said. Then he just stopped and stared and waited. I didn't think he was angry but I couldn't be sure.

"D'ye know'm?"

I shook me head.

"There's lots of old fellers at the Baptists. They don't do much. They don't bother with us anyway."

I was trying to think of something that might interest him.

"D'ye think there'll be a war, dad?"

I'd heard me mam and him talk about it quite a lot recently.

"Ah've no idea," he said. He didn't seem to have much interest in the matter today. "This Superintendent feller says he can't understand it."

Then he shut up again and looked at us as though he was waiting for some sort of explanation.

I was trying to think of a good'un.

"It seems he's got two lads at his Sunday School. They've both got the same name."

I looked blank.

"Same name as you as a matter of fact."

I shook me head in wonder and gave a little whistle as if to say it was surprising to hear that. But from the look on his face it wasn't enough. Me dad seemed to want a fuller kind of answer.

"Plenty of people with my name," I said. The words came out in a kind of gabble.

"Ah suppose so," me dad said. He smiled at us. I felt suddenly relieved. Then he looked puzzled. I knew me dad when he was like this.

"Mebbes they're brothers," I suggested.

Me dad nodded as if he'd just realised that might be the case. I wondered if I'd got away with it.

But then he said, "Well, Ah wouldn't think so. Ah wouldn't think their mam and dad would give their two sons exactly the same Christian name."

At least I kept on trying.

"Mebbes they're not brothers. Just two lads with the same name."

He wondered about that.

"Ye mean there's three of you at the Baptists with the same name?"

He sounded really puzzled.

I hadn't thought of that meself.

"Funny part about it," he said, "they've both got the same address. Ah say both but there might be three of them"

I shrugged me shoulders and tried to give the impression it was just some kind of unimportant mix up. Me mam was sitting at the table. She hadn't said a word, just kept looking at me and me dad whenever we spoke. But if I hoped for some kind of support from her, I'd another thought coming. She looked a bit frosty.

"Anyway," me dad said, "ye'd think Ah'd've noticed if there was two or three young lads 'cos they're all supposed to be livin' here. Ah would've seen them about the house. As it is Ah've only seen you."

He gave a little laugh.

"Ah mean, it's not as if they'd be inconspicuous. One of them has bright red hair. He's the Catholic."

McCracken.

"And would ye believe it," me dad said, "the other lad's black as the ace of spades."

But Ali was the only one I could get at short notice. He was the only one who'd do it for a penny. It was a big Sunday School. They always had more bairns there than they could ever get to know by name. I thought he'd just get his stamp and stick it in the Card. I didn't think they'd have time to notice him.

"The Baptist feller tells me he thinks that'un's a Mohammedan or something."

Probably. But I didn't know that mattered. His dad was a donkey man on the ships, I knew that much. They all lived down town, the Arabs.

Now me mam looked at us. She used the voice she sometimes used with me dad.

"And where've you got money from to throw around?"

She was worried about that. She needn't have been.

"Saved it."

All I'd had to do was put the knife in me money box.

She shook her head and I thought she hadn't believed us. But it wasn't that.

"Ah'm just sorry for those other two," she said. "What a disappointment for them. They were both looking forward to going. After all, they've both attended Sunday School."

I was going to say that McCracken had but that Ali had no right to go on the Outing. He'd only been three times. Before I spoke, she shut us up with a look.

"Poor Mrs McCracken," she said. "Fancy, she had no idea."

She looked across at me dad.

"She'd been horrified when she found that Attendance Card in his pocket. Ye know what the Catholics are like. They went to the chapel to see the Superintendent this morning."

For a moment she looked really angry as she turned to look at us.

"They're respectable folks. Regular Church goers," she said.

I could've made an answer but it wouldn't've got us anywhere so I just stood and waited. There was more.

"The Superintendent's going round to the other lad's house tonight. Going to have a word with his mam and dad. They'll be shocked as well."

They would.

All the parents would be shocked.

They'd all make a song and dance.

But parents could go to Ryton whenever they liked. If they wanted to, they could go to the Spanish City every week in life. What'd they got to be shocked about?

"And you're not going with the Baptists," me mam said. "Ye can go up there tomorrow and see the Superintendent and tell'm what ye've been up to."

So the next day I saw the Superintendent, told him what I'd been up to, handed over the Attendance Card. For a moment, I thought he was going to say it didn't matter, that he knew how important the Spanish City had been to us, that really he'd be happy for us to go with them.

But he didn't say anything like that. He just said, "Thank you. Goodbye. Don't do anything like that again."

I didn't get to the Spanish City that year. Maybe if I'd asked a bit later on they would've taken us. But I didn't dare ask and we didn't go. I got to Ryton with with the Methodists but it wasn't like the Spanish City. Nothing ever could be.

LOVE KNOT

Me Auntie Louie was all right really. Once you got over being hugged and kissed and generally smothered, she was really nice. And she always had a threepenny bit or a tanner for you. Me mam of course always said she was a star turn. But me dad. Well, he had his own views about me Auntie Louie.

"She's man mad," he used to say.

Or sometimes he would say, "She's daft as a brush, that lass."

But I think really he felt responsible for her. She was only nineteen after all. And she was his youngest sister and she had no other family.

Me mam and me Auntie Louie used to laugh at me dad behind his back. They used to roll their eyes and sigh and shake their heads. Well, that wasn't so bad. It was when they used to do it to his face that he used to get irritable. At least, I used to think that he was irritable. Mebbes he was just pretending.

One day I came in from school and me mam was very excited. She was all smiles and chattering away, loud as you like.

"It'll be lovely," she was saying. "Nice change for us."

Me dad concentrated on his plate. He didn't speak.

"We're all going to the pictures on Saturday afternoon. We're going up to Newcastle, to the 'Paramount'," she said. "With your Auntie Louie."

"All of wuh, mam?"

"Yes," she said. "You and me and our Maureen . . ." She broke off and pushed me dad's shoulder. "And him." She pulled a face at him but he wasn't having any.

"Aye, son," he said quickly. "All of us. And that includes your Auntie Louie's fancy man."

"Me Auntie Louie's got a fancy man?"

"Aye," me dad said.

"No," said me mam.

Our Maureen said nowt. I think she was wondering what it might be like to have a fancy man of her own.

"He's not a fancy man," me mam said. "He's a very nice gentleman. And he's a sailor. And he's got his captain's ticket."

I looked at me dad. I liked it when they were like this, me dad with a straight face, me mam indignant. Behind it all, they were laughing. You could see it in their eyes.

"Aye, well," me dad said, getting up from the table. "Ah'm sure he's a very nice gentleman." He began to smile. "What's his name?"

Me mam turned red.

"Haway," he said. "What's the feller's name?"

"You know," she said. "I've just told ye."

"Ah forget." And me dad starts sniggering.

"What's he called, dad?" I asked. I knew he was hoping I'd ask.

"What's he called?" he said. He opened great wide innocent eyes. "Ask your mam."

She seemed to bite on the word.

"What d'ye say, mam?"

"Gan on. Tell the lad. Speak plain."

"Horace," she muttered.

I mean, as if it was her fault.

But I laughed loudly to keep me dad company.

"And he's a very nice gentleman, is he?" me dad said.

He was sitting back in his chair, filling his pipe, and talking very casually.

"Yes."

He gave just a few draws on the pipe before he took out his matches.

"How'd ye know?" he said, as if he'd been thinking it over. "Ye've never met'm."

Me mam had no answer to that.

In those days the chips at the 'Paramount' used to be big and fat and golden and tasty. So was the cod. And the bread and butter was nicer than at home. And they had silver teapots with red hot handles. And waitresses. And round the walls great coloured pictures of film stars. Heaven. And we'd just seen 'Captains Courageous' with Spencer Tracy and Freddie Bartholomew.

Now that was a privileged childhood.

Anyway, me mam was laughing and chattering away and me Auntie Louie was done up in her best, all lipstick and powder and scent. And our Maureen was trying to act as if she was one of them. I was tucking in but me dad was very quiet. He only spoke when he had to. He wasn't unpleasant but I knew he was a bit quieter than usual. This Horace feller didn't seem at all like his name. He was big and handsome and strong looking. He laughed and joked with both the women and pulled their legs. You'd think he'd been a member of the family for years. He was just a bit cagey with me dad. And me dad was certainly cagey with him.

"Ye going back to sea soon then?" me dad asked Horace suddenly.

The smile left me Auntie Louie's face. She didn't like to be reminded of it.

"Aye," says Horace. "Ah'm gan down to the Med this time."

But he didn't seem to want to say any more about that. Perhaps he was considering me Auntie Louie's feelings.

"Oh aye," says me dad.

"That'll be nice," says me mam, trying to be agreeable and keep the ball rolling.

"How long ye away for, then?" me dad asks him.

"Couple o' months mebbes," Horace tells him. "Mebbes more." And he shut up like a clam again.

"Are ye likely to be captain soon? Get your own ship?" me mam asks.

"Oh aye," says Horace. "Ah've been first mate a while now." He blushed and gave a bit of a smile. Even to me he seemed to be a very modest sort of feller.

Me mam looks triumphantly at me dad but he just looks back and sniffs.

Our Maureen's goggle-eyed, of course, being in the company of a real live sailor.

It had been a smashing picture and then tea. A perfect day. I bet me Auntie Louie thought that as well. Only me dad looked a bit sour about it all. On the way home, when we'd left me Auntie Louie and Horace, me mam said something to him.

"Ah'm not miserable," he snapped at her.

"Ah hope you're not going to spoil things for your Louie," she said.

"Indeed not," I heard our Maureen say.

"Fine chance," me dad said.

Two weeks later on the Sunday, Horace and me Auntie Louie came to supper. Me mam had laid a nice spread on. Cold beef and potatoes, pickles, beetroot, dripping on your bread if you wanted it, trifle and lashings of tea. I don't know how she managed. She was a marvellous housewife. Me dad used to tell her that sometimes. Not often mind. But shyly and proudly when he did. But this night he wasn't passing any compliments. Not that he was in a bad temper or anything like that. In fact, he was very cheerful with Horace, asking him about his travels and his work on board ship and things like that. And as usual Horace didn't seem to want to say too much about all the places he'd been to and all the ships he'd worked on.

"We'll wash up if you boys want to talk," me mam said, when we'd finished, making on that Horace was already one of the family.

"You lazy devils just sit there and us girls'll do the work," me Auntie Louie laughed, entering into the conspiracy of easing Horace into our world.

"Just leave it to us," our Maureen said, keen to get her fourpennorth in. "A woman's work .... "

So off they went to the kitchen and we pulled our chairs up to the fire. We could hear the clatter of dishes, but the women were pretty quiet because they were trying to hear what we were saying. I think they thought they'd left Horace for a kind of test. Well, they had, I suppose.

"Here," says me dad, "Ah want ye to show us something."

He took a length of string out of the sideboard drawer and held it out to Horace.

"Aye?" said Horace. He was a little uncertain what he was supposed to do.

"Just show the lad here a bowline."

Me dad smiled, nodding first at the string in his hand and then at Horace and then at me.

"A bowline?"

Horace's jaw had dropped.

"Aye," me dad said, "a bowline."

Horace shook his head. "A knot, like?"

"Why aye, a knot," me dad said, laughing.

Horace put his hand to his brow.

"Ah've forgotten how to," he said. "Ah never do them now. It's just the deck hands what does them."

Me dad looked at him patiently. He was smiling away to hisself.

"Gan on, man. Have a try anyway."

"Ah can do a one, dad," I said, but he stared at us so

hard I didn't say anything more.

"Can't ye do it, Horace?"

There was a silence. Suddenly Auntie Louie poked her head in the room.

"All right, you lads?" she asked briefly, full of smiles.

"Aye," me dad said. He had a great grin on his face.

I nodded.

Horace went on looking at the string.

"Try a granny," me dad told him.

No response from Horace until he finally muttered, "Forgotten that'n an' all."

"And ye a sailor," me dad said, shaking his head.

"What about a reef knot?" I asked, ignoring me dad's look because I was feeling a bit sorry for Horace. I mean, everybody forgets things. "Try a one of them."

But Horace didn't move. He just stared into the fireplace.

Me dad looked over his shoulder, making sure me Auntie Louie and me mam weren't looking in. When he was certain they were still washing up, he turned back to Horace.

"Now, lad," he said. "Ah don't know for sure what your game is but Ah can guess."

Horace swallowed hard.

"She's an attractive lass and a good hearted one, our Louie," me dad continued. "But she's not got enough experience of the world."

Horace opened his mouth and shut it again.

"She's easily impressed."

Horace swallowed again.

"Ye've never been to sea, have ye? Ye've never got your captain's tickets," me dad said, keeping his voice low but managing to sound a bit nasty all the same. "The Shields ferry's about the only boat ye've been on."

Horace stood up very slowly. Somehow he didn't seem so tall all of a sudden; not so handsome either. And he certainly had nowt to say for hisself.

"Can ye let yourself out?" me dad asked.

He could. And did. Very fast.

And they hadn't even finished the dishes.

Of course, when they came back in, there was war on. Me dad was the villain of the piece. There was tears, near hysterics. As soon as I tried to tell them about the knots, I was sent up to bed, but I could hear it all, every word of it.

And then I heard the front door bang. Me mam went off with me Auntie Louie, to her house, and she spent the night with her.

Our Maureen said she'd go along with them. She was so upset for me Auntie Louie, she said, but me mam wouldn't let her so she had to stay in. I heard her go up the stairs to her bedroom. She never spoke to me dad or me.

Then later me dad came in to my bedroom. I think he might have been feeling a bit guilty. He sat down on the edge of the bed.

"How d'ye know he wasn't a sailor, dad?" I asked.

He seemed to struggle with the words as if he wasn't certain hisself.

"Why, he couldn't do the knots!" he said at last.

"Aye but, dad, what Ah mean is, before ye gave him the knots. Ye must've known. Had some idea, like."

"Oh aye," me dad said. He looked down at his hands. I think he was worrying about what me mam was going to say later. "Well, he didn't take much interest in 'Captains Courageous'. Ye know," he said, "that was a real sailor's picture, that was."

"It was, dad," I said. "It was smashin'."

"And anyway, another thing put us on the track," he said, a bit more confidently. He leaned towards us. "Ye never heard of a sailor called Horace, did ye?"

I thought a bit.

"Why, Nelson, like," I said. "He was Horatio."

"That doesn't count," he said stiffly.

Even when they were speaking again - properly I mean, not just grunting at each other - me mam and dad didn't say much in front of me. And I don't think they said anything in our Maureen's hearing. But it's funny what you can hear when you're a bairn.

"Your Louie's coming round tomorrow," I heard me mam say about a week later when I was supposed to be in bed.

"Ah suppose Ah'd better make meself scarce then," me dad said.

"No need for that. Ye'll have to face up to her sometime."

"Ah suppose Ah will," he said.

I could only imagine me mam smiling downstairs. Mebbes with a glint in her eye.

"She didn't really like'm anyway," she said at last. "Only you didn't have to poke your nose in."

"Why, you invited him here. There was all that palaver when the feller came here."

"Palaver, nothing."

"And ye went into the kitchen and left wuh alone."

"Well?"

"And there was all that song and dance when he went."

"Just, she didn't want you poking your nose in and interfering." Me mam was speaking to him as if he was a kid.

Me dad never did understand. And I didn't either. I'm not really sure me mam did if it came to that. Of course, our Maureen would have said she knew what was up if she'd been asked.

Anyway, me dad didn't interfere with the next feller me Auntie Louie found. He had bow legs, a huge Adam's apple and poppy eyes. He was an engineer. On the Shields ferry. He'd never been out beyond the pier. And he never had much to say for hisself. But, you know, it's funny. Me auntie married him and they worshipped each other for nearly fifty years.

VIRTUOSO

"Ye don't call that music."

Me dad nudged me shoulder hard so that me mam and our Maureen walking together behind could see him. I heard our Maureen give a snort. She was into high class music at that time and she had no patience with people who made remarks like that.

"Fat lot you know about music," me mam said.

"Ah know what Ah like," me dad said over his shoulder.

When we reached the kerb we all stopped together. It was the usual stuff with me mam and dad. They loved it of course. If she said white, you could be sure he'd say black. They stood at the kerb and grinned at each other.

But our Maureen was more serious about it. She would be.

"Some people just don't appreciate good music," she said looking down her nose. They were teaching to talk that way at the Convent School.

"That's right, pet," me dad said. If she was going to argue with him, it would be on his terms.

"Anyway," our Maureen says, sensing she's going to get no change from him on this particular tack, "it's not nice, talking that way about Mr Andolini."

"Ah've never said owt about Mr Andolini," me dad protested, his face innocent as a bairn. "Ah've never mentioned the feller." He opened his palms to the two of them. "When did Ah ever mention Mr Andolini?" he asked but neither me mam nor our Maureen bothered to answer. They just saw no traffic was coming and armed each other over the road in front of us.

Mind, me dad was a bit unfair. Mr Andolini had played very well. At least, the other seventeen people who had turned up to hear him seemed to think so. And they certainly seemed to like the tunes though they sounded a bit dull to me. Of course, if you weren't into old-fashioned violin music, it wasn't all that good. I wouldn't've gone to that kind of 'do' normally. And me dad wouldn't've been seen dead near one. In fact, I doubt if me mam and our Maureen would have gone if we hadn't found ourselves in the same boarding house as Mr Andolini.

Fancy, us in a boarding house. On holiday. It was the first time I'd ever been away from home. But one day me dad came and said to me mam, "It's your birthday. Ah've put a couple of bets on for ye. Ah've linked them."

Me mam sniffed. "Ah hope you've got something else for us. You never win anything." Which was true enough but then he didn't often back horses really. "What they called?"

"Ah forget," he said. And he blushed.

But when 'True Love' and 'Beautiful Lady' both came in first that day, he handed me mam a fistful of notes.

"Right," she said. "We're going to have a holiday this year. We'll go to Darlington. It's nice down there."

And that's where we went later in the year. And that was how we all got to talking to Mr Andolini.

He said he was a concert artiste and he was appearing in the church hall for two nights. Of course, me mam was wild with excitement. She wasn't only on holiday but here she was mixing with the likes of concert artistes.

She'd never met one before. And our Maureen, the world's worst pianist, was there jabbering away to him about Beethoven and Mendelsohn as if she knew them personally.

"Oh, we're here for a week," me mam was saying. "Down from Tyneside."

"On holiday?" says Mr Andolini. "Then you must come to my concert."

You should've seen me dad's face.

"Oh, lovely," shouts me mam. She was thrilled; she hugged herself; she beamed all round. "We're keen on music, ye know," she said. First I'd heard of it. She must have been affected by the holiday mood. After all I'd no idea what to expect. I'd never been as far south as Darlington before. When I first heard Mr Andolini speak I thought that must be how they talked in South Durham. It turned out, of course, he was Italian but a decent enough feller for all that.

So that night when we got back from the concert, we were still arguing among ourselves, me dad and me and me mam and our Maureen. Later on Mr Andolini came in.

"You enjoy it?" he asked. "The concert?"

You should've heard the two women glowing and crackling away. You'd think it was the best night out they'd ever had. Of course, me dad was polite to Mr Andolini and he told him he'd never heard anything like it before. When he said that me mam, and our Maureen for that matter, gave me dad a funny look.

All in all, Mr Andolini seemed quite satisfied with how things had gone at the concert but as me dad said later, you didn't get much butter on your bread playing the fiddle for just twenty people.

The next day our Maureen kept banging on about music and how wonderful it was, saying how she'd like to be a concert artiste, how she was going to practise and practise; promising she wouldn't have to be nagged any more about putting in half an hour a day.

"Don't you get lippy," she said to me when I told her I thought she practised too much already. She was chronic and she never seemed to get any better.

Anyway, when we went down to Darlington that morning our Maureen insisted on going into the big music shop right in the middle of town. She seemed to have found a new enthusiasm. She pulled me mam and dad over to the big pianos they had on show, Steinways or Bechsteins, one of those breeds anyway.

"Can I have a try?" she says to the feller in charge. She had a nerve. "I'm taking piano lessons."

"Oh aye," he says, very high and mighty in a posh suit. "Help yourself, pet."

So our Maureen steps up rather grandly, sits at the stool and crashes away at 'Chopsticks' and the scales and other old favourites till even me dad's embarrassed.

"That's enough now, Maureen," he says and he's heading for the exit and hoping we're all following.

But me mam's there, button-holing the feller in charge.

"Oh, we're all musical in our family," she's saying, and believing it too. She's giving him more or less what she gave Mr Andolini last night. I mean about us being musical. She had a canny enough voice herself but you couldn't say that of me dad. And our Maureen had just presented strong evidence that she wasn't a gifted musician. I certainly wasn't particularly musical. I might have taken to drums if I'd been asked. But I wasn't. Still, there was me mam going on without stopping about how musical a family we were and me dad stamping about with his hand on the door handle and our Maureen blushing with misplaced pride at her impromptu concert.

Then I saw those things in a box. They were a tanner each.

"Can Ah have a one o' them, mam?" I asked.

I'd seen them before. At home. But down here in

Darlington they seemed more romantic, more alien.

"Can Ah have a one?" I asked her again.

Me mam looked across at me dad. She seemed to have lost some of her enthusiasm. Her face was all twisted and desperate looking.

"He wants a kazoo," she said. She glanced down at me, a sort of imploring look in her eye.

"Why, get'm a one," me dad shouts over and then he drops his voice. "And let's get out of here," he says.

Well, out I came with me kazoo. A little tin submarine of an instrument that sounded like a top-flight comb and paper. What a noise it made. Not like any other instrument. I thought it made quite a thrilling sound.

Outside, me mam and our Maureen turned to me dad and me.

"We're going up to Binns' now," me mam said.

I knew what that meant. Trailing round looking at dresses and pots and pans and ironing boards.

"Do we have to, mam?" I asked her.

There was never a worse punishment than going to one of these big shops with me mam and our Maureen.

"No, son, ye don't," me dad said. "Ah'm not goin' with them. Ye can come with me."

So off we went, two men together. And he was great, on top form; we did laugh. About me mam and our Maureen and Mr Andolini and the feller in the music shop. And we had some sober thoughts too when we talked about Newcastle United's chances and how they compared with Sunderland.

"Ah'll only have a gill," me dad said late on in the morning. He jerked his thumb at the pub door. "Ah'll not be a minute, son. Stay there."

He looked up the street each way. If there'd been a toy shop or a sweet shop he'd have taken us in there first. Or he would have bought a comic for us. But there was nothing. Just offices; the Oddfellows Hall; the Congregational Church and a corset shop.

"Ah'll not be two shakes," me dad said. "Just ha'd

on."

I knew he wouldn't be long. We had to meet me mam in twenty minutes. If she thought he'd left us on the pavement outside a pub in a strange town - even if it was only half past eleven in the morning - she'd be really mad at him. She'd never forgive him that. I mean, left alone, in a strange town like Darlington anything could happen.

Me dad patted us on the arm.

"Play your thingummy," he said. He grinned. "Gan on. Play your whatyemaycally." Just out of daft he took his cap off and threw it on the ground. "See if ye can make a bob or two. Earn your keep."

He disappeared inside the pub and as he went I gave three rasping notes as loud as I could as a kind of fanfare. Then I saw him looking out of the window. He stuck his thumbs up and winked. Then he made a funnel of his fist and blew into it. He puffed out his cheeks and rolled his eyes and pretended to tootle away. Then he moved away out of sight to get his drink.

I loved it when he was in one of his daft moods. Overjoyed, really. And I put the kazoo to me lips and struck up a tune, looking, I suppose, quite as serious as our Maureen had when she played in the shop.

Then somebody touched me shoulder very gently.

"Hello."

I turned.

"Hello, Mr Andolini," I said.

He was smiling. He was such a kind-looking man. He had his violin case under his arm.

"Ah'm playing me kazoo," I told him.

"So I see," said Mr Andolini. "You're making music."

"Aye," I said and I blushed.

You'd think I'd given him a pound. He was delighted. I mean, a man like him, a concert artiste, and a bairn like me who knew less than nothing about music.

"Oh, you're a good family. You all love music," Mr Andolini said. Evidently he remembered what me mam had told him. Thank God he hadn't heard our Maureen play.

Suddenly he bent down and opened his violin case.

"I play with you," he said. "Now, boy, you blow soft. Ever so soft. And slow."

And there in the street, Mr Andolini played his violin and even though I didn't know one note of the blessed stuff from another, I knew that what I was hearing in those minutes was precious and beautiful. So I tootled away quietly in the background, soft and slow, and Mr Andolini's delicate notes danced their way up the street, soared over the walls, lifted beyond the buildings to the highest heavens over Darlington. And the people in the street stopped and listened and I think they knew that what they were hearing that morning was something they'd never heard before. Because that music was different. It seemed to be part of me and I was part of it. And I don't know, it was only minutes we played there, Mr Andolini and me, and mebbes he forgot all about it in a day or so. But it stayed with me, never left me. And me dad was there. He had come out of the pub and he was listening as well. And he was proud of us, I could tell.

Later, after me dad had managed to explain to the policeman that me and Mr Andolini weren't vagrants, when he'd persuaded him that we weren't beggars, when me dad had convinced him that he'd put the cap on the ground as a kind of joke, well, then, later, the three of us went to meet me mam and our Maureen.

"Ah've brought Mr Andolini along," me dad said. "Ah thought he'd like to have a bite to eat with us."

So we all went and had pies and peas at Carricks.

After all, Mr Andolini was a foreigner in a foreign land. Almost as much as we were, I suppose, down there in Darlington. Anyway, he enjoyed the afternoon with us. And we just felt we had to go to the church hall that night to hear Mr Andolini's second concert. And we went, the family of us, not just out of duty but because we really did like him. And anyway, at least as far as I was concerned, there was something in the music.

There was only fifteen people that night in addition to us four. And they really did appreciate his playing. And so did we. All of us. We thought that anybody who hadn't heard Mr Andolini play had missed something in their life.

Me mam and dad didn't even argue about the music on the way back. In fact they were very quiet. It was only when we got back into the boarding house that me dad started.

"Ah've always said," he announced, "the acoustics in those church halls is bad."

Our Maureen, sitting on the couch, sighed.

"Fat lot you know about church halls," me mam said. "When were you last in a church hall?"

She thought she had one over him there. But she hadn't really.

"Last night, pet," he said. "Listenin' to Mr Andolini. And tonight an' all."

He leaned back in his chair and took out his baccy pouch.

"But the acoustics there is perfect."

And he smiled across at her.

And she smiled back.

"And if Mr Andolini was playin' tomorrow night," me dad said, "Ah'd go an' listen to him again."

SHOW DAY

There was a few handy piles in the back lane, steaming away lovely. I dashed down to the coal house for the bucket and shovel and I could hear our Maureen calling for me mam.

"Mam," she's shouting, "Mam . . . he's off with the bucket and shovel again . . . Mam . . . he's got the bucket . . ."

What she meant was she was frightened some of her fancy friends from the Convent School would see us. But I was gone, tracking the rag and bone man or the firewood seller or whoever's pony had been so generous.

In a quarter of an hour I had a bucketful, brimming over, prime stuff, still warm.

"By lad," Mr Blenkinsop said when I came up his allotment path, "just the very feller Ah've been waitin' for."

He was delighted to see us.

And I was pleased meself. I'd obviously made a sale. He usually bought but he sometimes used to argue about the price. Today he was in such good fettle I was sure I'd get twopence for the bucket.

"No, son," he said. "Ah don't want no horse muck. Just put it down there and listen."

I put the bucket down.

"Now," he says and he puts his arm round us, "ye know what day it is th' day?"

"Aye."

"Well?" he said. "What day is't then?"

"Saturday, Mr Blenkinsop."

He took his arm away.

"Saturday, ye daft little bugger? Ah know it's Saturday, man."

He looked at us sadly and pushed his cap back on his head.

"It's Show Day," he said.

The Show. One of the great days. The Great Tyneside Flower, Fruit and Vegetable Show.

It was a big day for him. He always won prizes, cups and certificates. He used to get his picture in the 'Journal'.

He looked at us carefully as if he was making up his mind.

"Now," he said eventually, "Ah'm lookin' for a smart lad to give us a bit hand th' day."

He winked slowly. A gardener's wink, I suppose.

He must've seen the look in me eye.

"Ye're on then?"

"Aye," I said.

"Right," he said. "Now, Ah've got to gan down to the town. Ah've got to call in the hospital, like. See me daughter. She's had a bairn this morning. Ah've just been told."

He smiled this time to hisself. I wondered, did he want us to go with him? Get some sweets for the bairn?

"Now the difficulty is this," he said. "Look in here."

He opened the shed door. Inside there was spades, seed boxes, forks, canes, balls of string, dibbers, pots, sacks. Everything you could imagine. And there was a rickety old table and a chair with a pile of blankets on it. It was a tiny shed, stifling hot already and smelly in a gardening sort of way. We squeezed inside.

"There now," he said. He nodded at the table. "See them?"

There was two leeks on the table. They were huge. You'd never get them in a pot.

"Now, them's real leeks," he said. "Them's leeks ye dream about."

Well, they were big.

"Ah lifted them only this morning," he said.

Suddenly he put his head out of the shed door.

"Ha'd on a sec," he said, suddenly whispering. He went outside, up the path, to the gate. He looked up and down the cinder path. There was people working at all the other allotments but nobody seemed to be taking any notice of Mr Blenkinsop. He came back into the shed.

"Ah've been sleepin' here all this week," he said, pointing to the blankets. "Every blessed night."

I couldn't see why.

"Ye know what happened last year?"

I didn't know.

"Somebody come and pinched the buggers, that's what," His face was red with anger. "Pinched the buggers," he repeated. His mouth began to twitch. "Ye know why?" he asked and answered hisself straightaway. " 'Cos Ah've won first prize for leeks six times out of the last nine years. Best leeks. Biggest. Finest colour."

It seemed an awful fuss to me. I didn't even like leeks. If me mam ever made a leek pudding I could scarcely force it down.

"Ye know why Ah've got the best'uns?"

I shook me head.

"Ye don't? Ye don't know why mine's best?"

I had no idea.

"Well," he said, "it's no secret now. Ah've told somebody. All they need's a lot of attention. Good soil, water." Then he winked. "And my recipe."

His recipe? I knew all these leek growers had their secret recipes.

"Ah've never told nobody," he said. "Except one feller

that wheedled it out of us."

He sniffed and shook his head sadly.

"This feller was always nosin' about tryin' to find out how me leeks was so good."

He stared us in the eye.

"Keep off the booze, son. Ah wish Ah had. This feller bought us a few drinks, like."

And the secret was out.

"Now he's usin' the recipe."

I wondered what it was.

He seemed to be weighing up whether he dared to tell us and then he made his decision.

"Chocolate powder," he said. "And soot. Give them that all their lives. Ah'm not tellin' you the quantities, mind. Then the last three weeks is special."

He drew his breath in and looked over his shoulder to make sure no-one was hanging about outside.

"Every other day, ye pour on a bottle of Newcastle Broon instead of the water. A bottle for every five of them."

Outside there was a couple of rows of leeks. He must have poured out an awful lot of Brown Ale.

"Aye, but the part that takes the time's the ground glass."

"Ground glass?"

"Aye. Glass. Ground up fine as buggery," he said. "Course, ye don't put the glass on the leeks. Ye just grind it up and mix it in the Broon. It just gives an added something special to the mix."

I imagined him smashing old bottles and grinding the glass.

"It takes ages, mind, to get it really fine. And ye need three ounces of ground glass to every bottle of Broon."

I was amazed.

"Does it make them grow?" I asked him.

"Does it make them grow?" Mr Blenkinsop asked. "Make them grow? Why, look at the buggers." He pointed at the leeks. "Make them grow? Ah should think it bloody does."

They did look very big.

"But this feller's got the secret now." He scratched his chin. "Anyway, here." He dug into his pocket and brought out a two bob bit. "Here," he said. "Put that away."

Put it away? I'd already spent it in me mind.

"Now," he said. "Ah'm goin' off. You stay and keep an eye on them leeks."

"Just stay here?"

"Aye. In the shed. Don't bother about them ones Ah haven't lifted."

He nodded at the two rows of leeks. What a lot of Newcastle Brown, I thought. What a lot of chocolate powder and soot. And what an awful lot of ground glass.

"Just sit yasel' inside."

For a moment, a doubt crossed me mind. Something Mr Blenkinsop had said was beginning to nag away at us.

"D'ye think he'll come and try to pinch them?"

"Who?"

"Why, yon feller that came last year."

"Ah don't know. That's why Ah've been sleepin' here all week."

He sounded quite bad tempered as if I was being difficult or daft.

"Ye'll be safe. Ye'll be locked in. If he comes, take no notice. He'll never get inside. He won't dare do owt wi' you in there."

I wasn't so sure.

"Ah don't suppose the bugger'll come anyway. He wouldn't wait till Show Day."

I hoped he was right.

"Anyway, Ah'll be back soon. Ah've got to have me leeks in the Show Hall by four o'clock. That's the deadline. They're judgin' tonight."

In a couple of minutes he was gone. I watched him through the little window. When he'd completely disappeared, I felt very alone, locked in that little hut. I kept taking the two bob bit out just to reassure meself. Supposing the feller did come. Supposing Mr Blenkinsop forgot to tell me mam where I was. He'd promised to but he was getting old and he might forget.

Well, I sat and sat and as the morning went on the shed got hotter and hotter. Nothing happened for what seemed like ages. I had nothing to play with and nothing to read and in that cramped place I was almost too scared to move in case I disturbed the leeks. Champions've got to be left quiet and undisturbed.

Sometime late in the morning I heard the sneck go on the gate so I chanced a look out of the window. Would you believe it? It was our Maureen. She came mincing down the path as though she was visiting the poor.

"Are you in there?" she shouts when she gets to the door. She tries the handle.

"Are you in there?" she shouts again. "I know you're in there."

I didn't answer.

"The bucket's out here," she shouts. "I know you're in there."

She moved away from the door. Next thing I saw her peering through the chicken wire.

"Why don't you answer?" she said. She looked at us crouched under the table. "And you can get up from there," she said. "I can see you."

But I didn't say anything and I didn't stir.

She moved away from the window.

"He's here, dad," I heard her shout up the path.

Then I heard me dad's voice.

"What ye doin' under the table?" he said, looking at us through the chicken wire.

I had no answer but I stood up and went across to the window and looked at him.

"All right, are ye?" he asked.

"Yes."

"Ah've brought ye some sandwiches."

Good. I was starving.

"Mr Blenkinsop told us you were here. Said ye were on guard duty."

It was on the tip of me tongue to ask if he thought it was dangerous but I thought better of it.

"Can ye open the door?" he said. "Ah'll give ye the sandwiches."

"Mr Blenkinsop's got the key."

Our Maureen sniffed.

"Typical," she said.

"It's all right," says me dad. "Ah'll push them under the door."

It was a tight squeeze, mind. They didn't look much like me mam's sandwiches by the time I got them.

"There's a comic an' all," he said.

He pushed a 'Film Fun' through.

"Ye'll be all right?" he asked.

"Aye."

They went shortly after that. It was dinner time, they said. Sausage, bacon and onions. I watched them going down the path. They didn't even look back. I felt very lonely at that moment. But the comic helped.

As the afternoon wore on it got even hotter. And it was very quiet. From what I could see from the window everybody had gone home for their dinners. They'd all be off to the Show later. I wished Mr Blenkinsop would come back. He had a deadline to meet after all.

At about one o'clock I heard somebody else come through the gate. I looked out. It was a young feller. I'd never seen him before. He paused at the shed door and cleared his throat.

"Are ye in there, Mr Blenkinsop?" he said very quietly as if he was frightened somebody would hear him.

When he got no reply, he asked again, only a bit more loudly this time.

Then he tried the door handle. He said something or other to hisself and then I heard him walk round to the back of the shed. I thought I'd chance a look through the window in case I needed to shout for help. The place was still deserted.

Then a great bleary eye met mine, separated only by the chicken wire.

Then the feller gives a kind of squeal.

"Ye bugger, lad, ye didn't half give us a turn there," he said when he'd recovered.

"What d'you want?"

Me voice seemed to come from a great distance. It sounded very high pitched and nervous.

"Is he there? Mr Blenkinsop?" says the feller, straining his neck and trying to look into the inside corners of the shed.

"No."

"Comin' back, is he?"

I knew he couldn't see the leeks. I'd got me body between them and the window.

"No."

"Where's he gone?"

"To the Show."

"No he hasn't, man. He left here earlier without his leeks. Ah seen him."

I didn't answer. I didn't know what to say.

"Ah've come to collect them for'm. Take them to the Show."

He pressed his face hard against the wire.

"There's a deadline, ye know. Four o'clock. If he doesn't get them there in time, he's done for."

Still I didn't answer.

"So let us in, man."

I was desperate, trying to think what to say.

"They've gone," I told him.

"Gone?"

"Aye. Me dad came."

"Ya dad?"

"Aye. Ah gave them to'm."

The feller stopped a moment as if he was thinking things over.

"Got a key?"

"Who?"

"Why, you, man."

"No."

He stopped again, working things out. Then he gave a little excited sound as if he'd thought of something else.

"Has ya dad got a key?"

I didn't understand what he was getting at.

"No."

The feller gave a laugh.

"Why, if ye've got no key and ya dad's not got a one, how'd ye get the leeks out? 'Cos Blenkinsop's not got them 'cos Ah seen'm."

What could I say? He seemed very determined.

"Ah told ye," I said. "Ah gave them to me dad." I looked up as if I was trying to find an escape route through the roof. And that's when I saw it. There was a square crack of light in the roof.

"Ah put them through the trap," I said suddenly.

"Through the trap?"

"Aye," I said. "There's a trap door thing here. Ah stood on the table and handed them through."

He crouched down at the window and peered up at an angle so that he could see the crack of light.

"Has ya dad taken them then?" he asked at last.

"Aye," I answered. "He came at dinner time. He's takin' them down to the Show for Mr Blenkinsop. Ah'm just here learnin' about runnin' an allotment."

The feller didn't say anything else, just gave one more hard look at us through the window, then turned and went off down the path and out of the gate. You could tell he was disappointed.

And I'd thwarted him.

If he'd seen them, he might've barged his way in. I'd seen that happen scores of times at the 'Imperial'. But thanks to me, those leeks'd be at the Show tonight. And likely to win. I wondered exactly what Mr Blenkinsop would say. He'd be grateful, there was no denying that.

Later on, about two o'clock, me dad turned up again.

"Are ye thirsty, son?"

He had a bottle of lemonade.

"Aye."

"If Ah put the neck through the wire can you drink it?"

"Ah can do better than that, dad," I told him. "Simple."

I stood on the table taking care not to disturb the leeks. Then I eased off the square of wood in the roof. I levered meself up through the hole and stood on the roof. Me dad laughed and handed us the bottle.

"Your mam's sent ye a pie," he said. "She's kept ye some dinner as well."

And then didn't I tell him? There was this feller, I said. Talk about enormous. And very dangerous looking. He was going to barge down the hut but I talked him out of it.

Me dad listened and every now and again he said, "Getaway, now" and "Why, lad" and "Well, Ah never."

"If he'd come in, dad," I said and I told him for the umpteenth time what I'd have done.

As me dad left, I was still on the roof waving him off and still acting out how I would have dealt with the feller. For instance, if the door had fallen open, I'd've had to skip aside, then mebbes, as the feller came in ... or then, mebbes, I'd've taken a step backwards and just as he ... or supposing he'd run in, I might've jumped in the air first, just to puzzle him. So there I was on the roof, acting it all out, crouching, springing, taking steps back, forward ... a step here, a step there ... a step sideways ...

And then me foot slipped. And I sidefooted something.

Out of the corner of my eye, I saw the square piece of wood disappear through the hole in the roof. I heard the clatter as it hit the table and without looking I knew what I was going to see.

The table was all right. It had enough scars and gouges

and paint marks on it already. Nothing was ever going to spoil it. And the square piece of wood lay there on the floor but it didn't look as if it had suffered any damage.

But the leeks ....

I went straight home. I was cold and shivery even though it was a roasting hot afternoon.

I went in the back door and up the stairs. I wasn't sure who I wanted to tell. Somebody would have to find Mr Blenkinsop and tell him about his leeks. Last year he'd had them pinched; this year ....

Me mam was standing at the top of the stairs.

"Oh, here ye are," she says. "Here he is," she calls over her shoulder.

I went into the room. Our Maureen was sitting there smirking.

And me dad had a broad grin on his face.

And there was Mr Blenkinsop on the settee, but he was looking quite serious. He'd look more serious when I told him.

But before I'd a chance to say anything, he said, "Well, Ah've just come round to thank ye."

He nodded at us very cheerfully.

I tried to smile back and hoped I wasn't going to burst into tears.

"Ya dad tells me ye had a visitor," Mr Blenkinsop said, shaking his head angrily now. "Ah wouldn't trust that bugger." He looked up at me mam. "Pardon my French," he said.

"But Ah've got something else to tell ye, Mr Blenkinsop," I said.

And I told him. I left nothing out. One of them had a deep, three-inch gash in it and would be good for nothing but the pot; the other one he might be able to show if he could make sure he laid the damaged part down on the table. I'd brought them back, I told him. I'd put them out of sight in the coalhouse.

"Ah'm sorry," I said, really near to tears now. "It was an accident."

Not one of them stopped grinning. In fact, our Maureen burst out laughing.

"Trust you," she said. "Flea brain."

"Now then," me mam said. "That's not nice."

And me dad just said, "By lad," and started to giggle and laugh till the tears ran down his face.

And even Mr Blenkinsop laughed.

"No, son," he said. "Ye've done wonderful."

Wonderful?

"Them two leeks weren't likely winners. Too much green on them. Anyway, they weren't big enough." He waited for that to sink in.

"But Ah did sleep with them all the same. Stayed with them on that allotment all week. Took them up only this mornin'."

I couldn't understand - though it looked as if everybody else could.

"When Ah come back from hospital - and aye, the bairn's canny, a little lass - when Ah come back, Ah lifted the real ones and took them down and entered them. They're real beauties. And they've been grown in my back garden. And nobody knew a thing about them. That's why yon feller never come for them. He's been watchin' us all week at the allotment. Ye know," he said, glancing at me mam, "that bugger's had his eye on them leeks for weeks. Even them two down there in your coal house is better than his. Even in the state they're in."

Mr Blenkinsop sat back in his chair and smiled quietly to hisself.

"He'll never get a winner of his own. Wastes too much time," he said. "Spends his time messin' about with chocolate powder and grindin' glass up fine. And wastin' his money on Newcastle Broon. Ye know, Ah've told a few people that recipe over the years." He chuckled away to hisself for a bit. Then he leaned forward. "No bugger'll ever get my recipe," he said. "Not even you, son."

And he winked at us.

"Anyway," he said, "the judgin's at seven o'clock. D'ye want to come down?"

Well, I didn't. But me and me dad went just the same. And when Mr Blenkinsop picked up the cup - 'Best Leek: The Great Tyneside Flower, Fruit and Vegetable Show, 1939' - I felt I'd played some part in his victory.

And I never charged him for the horse muck.

FAMILY HISTORY

The flames on Mrs Elstob's chest always got the blame for what happened. At least as far as me dad was concerned. But then he never had a good word to say for Mrs Elstob or for her Norman who hadn't worked since 1928. Whenever Norman complained his leg was giving him gyp me dad used to say to me mam, "Well, it never lets'm down at openin' time. He's in there every night at six o'clock, leg or no leg."

But me mam was different; she always saw the good side of people, and, mind, you had to struggle if you wanted to see the good side of the Elstobs. But me mam always wanted to help. And the Elstobs were always there to be helped.

"Ah've never slept a wink all night, hinny," Mrs Elstob used to tell me mam. "It's the flames on me chest."

And me mam would say, "Oh dear, can Ah get ye something for it?"

Trust me mam.

"There's no betterness for the flames," Mrs Elstob would tell her. "Unless ye've gorra bowl of soup ye could let us have." Or it might be a bottle of milk or a slice of ham even. And then Mrs Elstob would go back into the house, put her head under a towel and snoke up fumes of Friar's Balsam by the hour.

Not that I knew much about it. I didn't know then how much the Elstobs scrounged off me mam - twists of tea, sugar, margarine, anything she could give. Money, possibly. I don't know how me mam could afford to give anything away. What I do know is she never let on to me dad.

But for me there were more important things to think about. Especially one Wednesday morning that late summer when, hard up as they were, me mam and dad gave us a bike. They'd saved for it and there'd been some money left over from me dad's win on the horses earlier in the year. The bike wasn't new but to me it was beautiful. I thought of it every waking hour, rode it every possible minute of the day. On the Friday morning I was still wobbling about and falling off. Then, as if by magic, I mastered it. When I was called in at seven that night, I was a free-riding spirit. On the Saturday I was practising skids and riding with no hands. Course, our Maureen was out in the back lane, spying on us.

"I'll tell dad and mam if you don't use both hands," she kept saying. Or, "You'll ruin the tyres doing that. I'm going to tell."

At about half past ten on the Sunday morning, when I was planning a career as an international cyclist, I heard our Maureen shouting to us again.

"You'll have an accident on that bicycle," she said in her best Convent School voice. I think she was jealous of us. She'd got her bike two years before.

"Anyway," she says, "you have to be back here in twenty minutes."

"What for?"

I didn't want me training interrupted.

She closed her eyes and stuck her chin out, the way she did whenever she was trying to throw her weight around with us.

"Dad says. He wants you back. Don't be late, he says. Anyway, it should be obvious why he wants you."

It wasn't obvious to me but there was no point in arguing.

So at about ten to eleven I was leaning me bike on the back lane wall. I didn't want to be late because I was trying to please me mam and dad because they had been good to us. I mean, you don't get a bike every day.

"Wotcheor, son. We're just poppin' over to see ya mam."

It was Norman Elstob. Him and Mrs Elstob were coming out of their back door.

"The battery's gone on the wireless," he said. "We're goin' over to listen to yours."

Norman limped over and stopped in front of the bike. He hadn't seen it before. He said nowt at first and he gave it the once-over as if he was an expert. He stood back and eyed it and then crouched down and inspected the wheels. Then he stood up again and nodded to hisself as if he was well satisfied.

"By, lad," he said at last. "A Horculees, eh?"

He stroked the handlebars. Then Mrs Elstob came over to look at it.

"Ee, it's lovely, pet," she said. "A Hercewles, eh?"

Just then, me mam came to our back door.

"We're just havin' a look at the bike here," Norman said. "By, he's a lucky bairn." He turned to me. "By, you're a lucky lad with a mam and dad like what ye've got."

Me mam blushed with pleasure. Before she had a chance to say anything, Mrs Elstob cut in.

"Can he gan a message for wuh?"

Me mam hesitated. She never liked to be thought unwilling to help but I knew she wanted us in the house.

"It'll only take'm a minute on the bike," Norman said quickly. "Just up to Hardin's. No time at all on a bike like this'n."

"Aye, mam," I said. I liked the idea of going a message on the bike. "It'll not take us a minute."

"Worra good bairn," Mrs Elstob said before me mam

had a chance to answer. She pushed a coin into me hand. "Just a bottle of Friar's Boslum." She turned to me mam. "It's the flames again, hinny."

"And five Wood's for me. And a bottle of Newcastle Broon." Norman rubbed his hip. Obviously his leg was giving him real gyp that day.

"Make sharp then," me mam said. She looked a bit anxious.

Up at the corner shop I was the only customer. But old Harding only went one speed. He rummaged round in near dark in a tangle of skipping ropes, bundles of firewood, patent medicines, kippers.

"Friar's what?"

"Boslum."

He shook his head. He was the sort of feller who'd rather not sell you anything.

"Who's it for?"

I told him.

"Hm."

At last he found a bottle, right back on a dark shelf.

"And five Woodbines, please."

"Ah don't sell tabs to bairns," he grumbled. "Who they for?"

I told him.

He said something to hisself and shook his head again.

At last he gave us the tabs.

"Ah don't sell beer to bairns either," he said when I asked him. But I got it all the same.

Shortly after eleven I was home, charging up the stairs. The messenger had carried out his mission.

It was quiet in the kitchen. Me dad sat scowling at the wireless. Our Maureen was staring at the wall, thinking great thoughts. Me mam said nothing, just took the balsam and the beer and the cigarettes and handed them to the Elstobs. I could see she was a bit on edge.

"Very kind," Mrs Elstob said.

"Much appreciated," Norman said.

They looked so cheerful. And then suddenly me dad stood up, towering over them.

"Ha'd on," he said. "Ha'd on now."

I could tell he was angry. Not the way he used to be angry if me or our Maureen did anything wrong though. It was a different sort of anger.

"Now, then," me mam began to say.

"You an' all, missus," he said. "Just be quiet, will ye?"

I'd never heard him speak so sharply to me mam before.

"Now," me dad shouted, pointing at the Elstobs. "You two get out of this house. Ah'm sick of your hangin' about here. Ah don't want ye in here again. Ever."

The Elstobs just looked bewildered. You'd have thought they would say something. But they turned and went out without a word. I couldn't understand what was happening.

Me dad followed them to the top of the stairs.

"Bugger off," he shouted after them. He'd worked in the shipyards all his life but he didn't normally swear at home.

"The boy should've been here," he yelled after them, louder than ever. "He should've been here. Thanks to you two he wasn't."

He came in and went over to the window, looking down into the back yard. For a bit he never said anything and none of us spoke. I'd never seen him so angry.

Then it was just as if he was speaking to hisself.

"He should've been here," he said again.

And I should have been there. I should've been there with me mam and dad and Maureen. There to hear Chamberlain. To hear him say the words "... and consequently, this country is now at war with

Germany ..."

Me dad wanted us there in front of that wireless. He hadn't said anything beforehand, hadn't given his eleven year old son any warning. He just wanted him there at that time. On that great occasion. To hear it. Feel history happen.

And that boy would've been there, would've heard it, if it hadn't been for the flames on Mrs Elstob's chest and for Norman's beer and baccy.

"And the bike," me mam used to say later. "If you hadn't got him the bike. That was you. The bike was your idea. If he hadn't had the bike ...."

Ever after me mam defended the Elstobs, though they never came to the house again; me dad, of course, never wavered and always blamed them. And never forgave them.

Nobody ever thought of blaming Adolf Hitler.

ONLY THE VALIANT

You know how in the cowboy pictures the hero says he'll fix the bad feller. Alone. Well, it was just like that with me.

"Ah don't care," I'd said. "Ah'm not frightened of'm."

Everybody'd stopped talking. They were trying to decide if I was lying or boasting. Or both.

"Not afraid of'm?"

"No. And Ah'm not afraid to tell'm."

"Not afraid of Dodger?"

They couldn't believe it.

By, I was proud of meself. After all, I was just about the youngest. They were nearly all twelve or thirteen. I was only eleven. And small for my age. But I stuck out my bottom lip in defiance. Remember Buck Jones? Well, just like him. But I knew that in the end they'd talk us out of it. They'd laugh at us and eventually I'd join in the laughs against meself. But they'd think I'd been pretty brave, considering.

"Oh well, mebbes you're right. Mebbes Ah am a bit afraid," I would say. "S'natural enough."

And I'd admit I was just as frightened of Dodger as they were.

"Mebbes Ah wouldn't have much chance," I was

going to say, "him bein' so big."

That's how it would end. And for me, exit with honours.

Except that day, it didn't go like that. Except that day, I was so worked up, I began to believe meself. I ignored all their jeering and laughs. I was carried away. I wouldn't back down. I couldn't.

"Prove it then."

A different tone. I knew who that was. I knew Charlie Bennett's voice. I'd never liked him. Especially now. He was one of those big show-offs and he was about fourteen.

"Prove it," he said again. "Gan up to'm. Tell'm you're not frightened of'm. Gan up to Dodger and tell'm that. Face to face."

The others weren't laughing any longer. They'd stopped jeering. They were like Bennett. They were serious now.

"Aye, gan on then," they called out. "Gan up to Dodger. Tell'm he doesn't frighten ye."

Did they really think I was daft enough to do that? Did they really think I was going to walk up to Dodger and say to him, to his face, that he didn't frighten us? Madness. Dodger frightened lads two and three years older than hisself. And he was two years older than me. What was I letting meself in for?

I mean, when he came along the corridor, you tried not to look at him; in the school yard, you always hoped he'd be seeking somebody else; if you saw him in town, you turned back, ran up side streets, climbed walls. Anything to get out of his way. And if he did catch you, if he wasn't immediately attending to somebody else, it was likely you'd get a punch on the chest or a kicked shin or a Chinese burn or half-nelson or even a full one. And if he had time on his side, you might get all of them.

"Course Ah can prove it," I heard myself say. And I couldn't believe that I was saying it.

So the next week, I spent me time looking out for

Dodger and looking out for meself. I managed to keep away from him. But I knew it couldn't go on for ever. And Bennett was having such a smile to hisself whenever he saw me. And so were some of the others.

"We'll go down this week-end and get ye a new mac."

I was just at the age when I never wanted to be seen in the street with me mam. You never saw John Wayne out with his mam, did you?

But she said I needed a new mac.

"We'll go to Burton's on Saturday," she said very firmly.

"Ah'll meet you there, mam," I told her.

"Oh, listen to him," our Maureen said. My clever sister, two years older than me and sounding more superior and grown-up by the day. Recently she'd been growing out of her sweaters at the front and she used to argue with me mam about this. It was all beyond me, of course. I was more concerned with Hopalong Cassidy and Hoot Gibson.

"Ah'll meet y'outside," I said, ignoring our Maureen.

"You'll come with me." Me mam gave us one of her looks.

Over in the corner, me dad lowered his 'Journal'.

"He's growin' fast, that lad," he said. "Make sure it's the right size."

By which he meant I needed a mac to fit a lad several inches taller and two or three stones heavier than I was.

Me dad went on talking to hisself behind the paper.

"Lads grow fast," he was saying.

"That's the one," me mam told the man in Burton's.

I'd given up saying it was too big.

"Put it on," she said. "Wear it home. It'll give it an airing."

"Just needs the sleeves rolling up," our Maureen

sniggered. "And a tuck in the back." She paused, then added, "And a six inch hem."

"That's enough," me mam said. "He looks very nice in it." She nodded her approval.

Walking home, I wondered if it could be worn like a cape. If I took me arms out of the sleeves and fastened the neck button, like the feller in 'The Mark of Zorro' .... but then I heard the laughter and remarks from behind.

"By, he looks nice, doesn't he?" I heard somebody shout.

"Where's the fire been?" somebody else called out.

There was three of them; Charlie Bennett and two others. They grinned and ran to catch us up.

"Introduce us to your friends then," me mam said, looking fairly stern, as if she was daring them to go on with their scoffing.

Bennett smirked his oily smirk, putting hisself out to be pleasant. And so did the others. You wouldn't believe it. In no time at all me mam had warmed to them. So had our Maureen. When we left them, I knew the lads had made a good impression.

"He's a nice looking boy, the tall one," Maureen simpered, gazing back at Bennett.

"He is," me mam agreed. "And lovely manners."

Nice looking? Lovely manners? Bennett? Trust them to like him. Might as well have fancied Dodger.

"Ye think he's good lookin', ye want your eyes testin'," I muttered.

"What's his name again?" our Maureen asked. "I didn't catch it."

"No, Ah didn't," said me mam, smiling fondly. "Such a nice type of boy." She looked hard at me. "Ah like a boy with nice manners," she added pointedly. "What's his name?"

Well, I wouldn't tell them his name. If they wanted to know, they'd have to find out for theirselves. I'd had enough of a putting-up that afternoon.

Then, to cap it all, when me mam couldn't hear her,

our Maureen said, "At least, whatever his name is, his coat fits."

It was the last straw. I was furious and there and then I swore I'd get me own back. I'd have me revenge. At least, if I wasn't too busy in the next few days keeping out of Dodger's way.

Dodger, I thought. Bennett. Our Maureen. Nowt but problems. But it came suddenly, right out of the blue. A solution. I didn't go in for romantic films. Not my style at all. But there was one ... I couldn't say what it was or who was in it ... but the plot, I hadn't altogether forgotten ....

"Like to meet'm?" I said to our Maureen.

Me mam was in the scullery washing up; me dad was checking the results in the 'Sporting Pink'; and Maureen was clearing the table.

"What?" she frowned, looking at us suspiciously.

"Ah can arrange it, ye know," I told her. "Easy as owt."

She pretended she wasn't sure. Then she shook her head.

"Course not."

"Write'm a letter. Ah'll give it to'm at school on Monday."

"No." She blushed. "I'm not doing that. I'm not writing to him."

"Go on," I urged her. "He's a good lad. You'll really like'm."

I could see I was having an effect. She was smiling to herself and fluttering her eyelids. I talked to her for quite a while. It was easy.

"Well," she said eventually. "I might. I'll see. I'm not sure."

She began to concern herself with the pattern on the tablecloth.

"Anyway," she said. "I don't even know his name."

I smiled. "Oh, we just call him Dodger. Harold Dodgson's his real name."

"I don't know," she said, as much to herself as to me. "I'll see."

In the corner me dad was muttering to himself.

"We haven't won the pools again, son," he said as if he was surprised.

On the Monday morning I was in school early. As a senior milk monitor, I could go in the building from half past eight. I found Dodger's classroom and put the note on his desk.

"At the pictures," I told our Maureen when I got home. "He'll see ye outside tomorrow night at six o'clock."

On Tuesday night, I waited opposite the 'Imperial', standing deep inside the shadow of the hardware shop door.

Over the road Dodger was by the kiosk. He'd asked some questions round the school after reading Maureen's note. And he was pleased with what he'd heard. For why else had he been here so early, in his best suit, his hair flattened down with 'Attar of Roses'? He was obviously nervous, looking up at the clock every few seconds. He started to pace up and down. She was late. He was worried.

Then he saw her. He stiffened and ran his hand across the top of his head to make sure the crown wasn't sticking up. He tugged at his jacket, then walked towards her.

He smiled.

Our Maureen smiled back.

And walked past him. Actually walked straight past

Dodger.

I heard him shout, "Hey. Come here. Aren't you the lass .... ?"

I couldn't hear what else he said but our Maureen looked alarmed. She stopped still. He went up to her. They spoke for a short time. Then, they both turned and went their separate ways home.

And in the shadows, I laughed.

On the Wednesday morning, I didn't try to hide from Dodger. In fact, I sent one of the lads to fetch him. Anyway, I knew he'd be looking for us.

"Tell'm Ah'm waitin' here for'm," I said.

While I waited in the middle of the playground, I sensed everybody knew what was up. I'd called out Dodger and the lads were gathering in small groups, just waiting.

And then Dodger came, walking slowly across the playground. He was huge, menacing, frightening. But it was too late to run.

"Okay, Dodger," I said, speaking pure, measured Gary Cooper. "Keep it nice and quiet. Ah'll say nowt if you say nowt. So just turn round, walk away and keep on walkin'. Nice and easy."

I was relaxed with just the suspicion of the coiled spring about us. Everybody's eyes were on us, all wondering, admiring. They couldn't hear what I'd said because I'd kept me voice low and anyway, none of them had dared to come too close.

"Say nowt? Say nowt about what?" Dodger was puzzled.

I narrowed me eyes, gave him a crooked smile.

"About last night, Dodger. How you looked so daft standin' there and bein' stood up."

"Oh," Dodger said, nodding as he began to understand what this was about.

"Ye had ya best suit on. And ya hair was a bit smarter

than it is now. But Ah'll keep quiet if you're sensible."

Dodger licked his lips. I gave him a level stare.

"Just walk away," I told him, just a hint of menace in me voice. "Nice and easy, pardner."

Around about, nobody moved. They were astounded. At last, Dodger had met somebody who wasn't terrified of him.

"A man's got to do ..." I said in me easy drawl, not mocking him, giving him the chance to back off with dignity.

That was when he hit us.

It could have been a brawl of epic proportions. I could have thrown him through a window; he could have slammed me against the wall; a door could have fallen off its hinges; we could have traded blow for blow, each one landing squarely on the chin. It could have lasted for ages. At the end, we could have staggered towards each other, faces bloody, clothes torn, scarcely able to throw another punch.

But it wasn't like that.

After that one punch, I couldn't get up. Dodger stood over us for a while as if he was wondering whether to force us to me feet. But in the end he didn't. He just grunted, eyed the circle of lads, and walked away.

I got no sympathy at home.

"Serves you right," Maureen said, even though she didn't know who'd hit us. Or why. "I expect you were playing the fool as usual." She was pleased and made no attempt to hide it. She hadn't forgotten last night.

"Stop fussing, it'll be all right," me mam said. "Put this wet flannel on it. It'll go down in no time."

"Ah hope you stood up for yourself," me dad said round the side of his 'Chronicle'.

"Oh, aye," I told him. "Ah gave'm as good as Ah got."

Funny. After that Dodger calmed down, became quite the model schoolboy. I don't know why. Just growing up, I suppose. Pity I hadn't shut me mouth just a bit longer.

NO FUNNY BUSINESS

"Ye can stop that bubblin'," me dad said. "Ah can't abide lasses bubblin'."

Our Maureen took no notice. She just curled up on the settee and went on crying. Every time we thought she'd stopped she would suddenly start up again. And every time after me dad had snapped at her, he'd shrink down behind his paper. Trouble was, he was one of those big tough fellers who didn't know what to do when a lass burst into tears. The only thing he did know was that if he didn't look out he'd be agreeing to whatever it was she wanted.

"Now it's no good," he said, trying to sound very fierce and looking very stern. "Ah'm not the sort of father that gives in just like that."

Our Maureen lets out a wail, timing it perfect for me mam who's just coming in the door.

"What's on here?" me mam says. She's been down to see me Auntie Louie and she's come in soaked. It's pouring outside. All she wants is a nice cup of tea, not a daughter blaring her lungs out and a husband looking miserable. At least I was all right. In fact I always enjoyed it when our Maureen couldn't get her own way.

"It's dad, mam," our Maureen shrieks. "He won't let

me go to ......" and the rest of the words were lost in so many tears and sniffs that you'd think she'd been saving them up for days.

"What's the matter?" me mam says, struggling out of her mac. She gives me dad a dirty look as much as to say, "Can't Ah just slip out for a couple of hours without you getting the house in an uproar?"

"No use lookin' at me like that," me dad grumbled. "She wants her own way, that's her trouble."

I was just on the point of agreeing with me dad. I was going to say it was that Convent School that was at the root of it but me mam turned to me. She wasn't smiling.

"Time for bed, you."

Usually I would have said, "Do I have to?" or "Can I stay up a bit later?" but I thought that would get our Maureen off the hook. Anyway, I wanted to be in me mam's good books. I'd seen a pair of football boots in the second hand shop. They were scarcely worn. Somebody'd snap them up shortly, I was sure of that.

"Right, mam," I said. "Ah'll go up now."

They'd never seen us go to bed as quickly as that. I think there was a moment when somebody was going to say, "Hey. Hold on. Don't go yet. Ye've got half an hour's arguin' left." But I went. I could hear everything if I kept my bedroom door open anyway.

For the first few minutes though, all I could hear was our Maureen bleating on, accusing me dad, pleading with me mam.

Me dad was saying things like:

"Ye can't always have your own way"

or

"She can't always have her own way"

or

"Ah don't always get my own way."

But I knew pretty soon which way the wind was blowing. I could tell by me mam's voice she was getting more and more on our Maureen's side.

"It's a social accomplishment," I heard her say.

"To blazes with a social accomplishment," me dad said in the voice of a man who knew he was going to be beaten in the end.

"Ah went to dances," me mam said. "When Ah was young Ah went."

And then I heard her say, "No, Ah wasn't different."

Then she said, "Well, Ah met you at a dance."

Then she told him that if he'd known then how to dance they might have got on better that first time.

"You were hopeless. Your feet were all over," she told him. "They still are when ye come to think of it."

Then she really let him have it.

"Ah was only fourteen then. Same's our Maureen," she said. "And your Louie was going at thirteen."

Dad defeated, ten nil.

At least, in a way he was.

"Things are different now," he was saying. "She can go to the school dance. Ah don't mind that. It's these dancin' classes she's on about. She can't come back from there by herself at all hours of the night. And it's blackout."

I heard our Maureen whining from the settee.

"The classes finish at eight," she shouted.

"That's enough," I heard me mam say to her. "Don't talk to your dad like that."

"You can't go over there every week to sit in a class with her for an hour," me dad said to me mam, trying to sound reasonable.

"No," she agreed. "Ah can't."

"Well?"

"And you can't either," she said to him.

"No. That's what Ah'm sayin'."

"Yes, but .... , "me mam said.

And that's how I was roped in to take our Maureen to dancing classes every week for the next six weeks. Until her school dance.

I would've resisted. You wouldn't've caught me going to dancing classes. And our Maureen didn't seem to keen on the idea.

"Him?" she said. "He's going?"

"He'll look after ye," me dad said.

"Couldn't look after a flea," she said.

"Ah well," me dad said, "you're not a flea. He's goin' or you're not."

"Huh."

You can't blame me for not being over enthusiastic. But those football boots were in the second hand shop.

"We'll see," me mam said, when I mentioned them.

All right, I thought. But there'd better be some kind of reward. I mean, dancing classes. For a lad like me. Wasn't normal.

The first night our Maureen made us sit on another seat on the tram. I was three or four places behind her.

"I'm not sitting with him," she told me mam before we went. "Not in public."

But she had no way of getting rid of us after that. I walked with her, well, a couple of paces behind, to the house where the classes were held.

"Come in, hinny," an old woman said when Maureen knocked at the door. She stood aside and Maureen went on upstairs. "Is the bairn with ye?" she shouted.

"Yes," our Maureen said without looking round. She didn't sound too pleased to admit it.

Anyway, I followed her upstairs to a big room with no furniture in it, except for a table with a wind-up gramophone. There was brown lino, polished to make it easy for the dancers. There was about fifteen of them, mostly girls, a few lads, between eight and fourteen. The old woman handed us over to another woman who, I suppose, was her daughter.

This woman, Pauline, who took over, told us how marvellous it was to learn to dance and what fun it would be.

"And have any of yez danced before?" she asked.

Some of them had. They put their hands up and giggled. Our Maureen was one of these.

"And you haven't, pet?" Pauline asked me.

"No."

"But you're going to have a good try, aren't ye?"

I hadn't come for that.

"Ah'm her escort," I said, pointing at Maureen. "Ah'm here to look after her. Me dad says."

The others had turned round and were staring at us. I felt meself going red. Some of them were whispering now. I was beginning to feel silly.

"But you're going to join in with them, aren't ye?" Pauline asked.

"No," I said. And if I'd dared I would have run out.

Pauline just shrugged and looked at our Maureen. She rolled her eyes, and put her finger to her temple. Everybody laughed but I just scowled at them.

Anyway, they started their dancing. They all took part. I just sat at the side.

"Left foot, right, together, now le—-eft," Pauline's trilling away to a record of Debroy Somers and his Savoy Orpheans. "Lovely. Careful now. Left foot, right, together now ....."

It went on for ages. I hated it. I felt that they were all looking at me, the only one sitting down. I thought it would never end. Then, when it did, our Maureen comes over to us.

"Get the coats," she says, quite the royal lady.

Well, I did. But only because I was in a hurry to get out and home. So I didn't argue. Anyway, the coats were easy enough to come by in a little cupboard at the top of the stairs.

"See yez all next week," Pauline's shouting to everybody, and smiling as though everything had been wonderful. Except when she came to me, her smile seemed to fade. "See you next week?" she asked but she'd have been glad if I'd said I wasn't coming.

"Yes," I said. "But Ah don't want to come."

But I don't think she heard.

Anyway, I'd got to the bottom of the stairs and out into the street, but our Maureen was taking some time. She was coming down the stairs and laughing and putting her head first on one side, then on the other, as if she wasn't right. A lad she'd had a dance or two with was talking to her. When they came out, they took no notice of me, just went on talking and walking up the street.

"Ah'll set ye home," says the lad. He must have been nearly fifteen. I couldn't understand it, a lad his age going to dancing classes.

"Are you sure?" asks Maureen. "It's a long way."

"Oh, no. Not for me," says the lad. "It's no bother. A lass could get lost in the blackout, ye know."

So far they'd ignored me. I wasn't putting up with that.

"We're going on the tram," I told the lad. "It'll cost ye fourpence return."

He shrugged his shoulders.

"That's all right. Ah've got plenty money."

Our Maureen looked at him in admiration.

So he came, this lad Barry, up to the tram, all the way back home, me sitting seats away from them. Finally I followed them back to the end of the street.

"Ah'd better go now," he said. He was talking as posh as he could to impress our Maureen. He didn't impress me.

"Right," she says.

"See ye next week?"

"Yes."

I was just hanging round like Toss Willie, listening to all this. It was getting cold and they seemed to be in no hurry.

"Time to go in," I reminded her.

"You go on," she said.

"No fear. Ah'm your escort."

I wasn't going to let their daft carry-on get in the way

of a pair of football boots.

"Daddy won't mind," she said.

Daddy?

She'd never called him Daddy before. I think she'd seen a film with Ann Todd or Celia Johnson the week before. Anyway she was putting on the tongue.

"Aye, he will mind," I said. "He said you weren't to be on your own in the blackout."

If looks could kill.

But she was in the house soon enough.

Well, the next few weeks I went to the class. Same pattern as the first time. Walking to the tram, me in front or behind; the tram and again in different seats; the old woman and Pauline and the jokes at my expense; then this lad Barry coming back with us.

Anyway, one night, Barry came up to me as soon as we arrived. Our Maureen was having a bit chat with some of the lasses so over he comes. I didn't like him at all. I didn't know why our Maureen thought he was so good. Even I could see all the great fat spots on his neck. Every week he'd kept making jokes about me sitting on me own and about how I must be frightened of lasses. But I wasn't. It's just I didn't think they were as good as lads. And dancing wasn't for lads anyway. Seemed daft to me.

Anyway this night he was all smiles.

"Wotcheor, kidda. All right, are ye?"

"Aye, canny," I said.

"Ye don't need to stay, ye know," he said. He was whispering and sort of glancing over to the other side of the room where our Maureen was jabbering away, putting on a bit of a show for this Barry. She was talking to some other lasses but she kept sneaking looks across at him.

"At the end, you just gan home by yaself, son," he said. "Ah'll bring her."

I shook my head.

"Gan on, man," he said, still trying to smile.

"No."

I was stubborn as they make them. I'd been given a job to do and I was going to do it. Especially if he was asking favours.

"She'll be all right, ye know," he said. "Ye needn't worry."

"Ah'm not worryin'. Ah'm goin' home with her. Me dad says."

He starts to swing his shoulders round as if he was inventing a new dance.

"Haway, man," he says. "Giz a break."

"No."

He drew a deep breath.

"Ah'll tell ye what," he says. "Ye know me dad?"

"No."

"Ye do."

"Ah don't"

"Ye do, man."

I wasn't going to say I did when I didn't. But I wasn't going to go on arguing so I just shut up and looked at him. He turned his head to look at our Maureen and shrugged his shoulders. She gave me a very nasty look. Then she looked back at Barry and nodded as if to say, "Have another go".

The lad looked absolutely hopeless. He'd gone bright red.

"Me dad's got the second-hand shop," he said suddenly.

"Has he?"

"Aye."

I didn't twig what he was on about.

"Ye know the one?"

"No."

"The one with them football boots," he said. "Your Maureen told us you'd been talkin' about them."

Those football boots? That second-hand shop?

"Ye know now, don't ye?"

I did.

"Ah'm in there on a Saturday," Barry said. "Ah look after it on a Saturday when me dad gans to the match. Ah'm in every Saturday."

Was he?

"Ah can settle prices sometimes."

Could he?

"Like, them boots is half a crown."

Didn't I know it?

"But, mebbes if a lad come in and could only afford a shillin', well, mebbes, ye know ...."

Oh, I knew all right.

"Ten minutes," I said. "But Ah'll come back with ye both as usual. But when we get to the street end, Ah'll walk up towards our house. Ah'll do that. But you and our Maureen have to stand on the pavement edge. No funny business. Ten minutes, that's all."

So there I was, crouched under a privet hedge not a hundred yards from home and there they were, in full moonlight on the pavement edge, about forty yards away. I just hoped nobody came out of our house. There'd be war on. Or if somebody came up the street who knew our Maureen. What would they think of her? And what would they think of me? And if they told me mam and dad, there'd be no boots.

Anyway, nobody came by. And after what I thought was ten minutes I gave a shout.

"Time's up. Haway in."

For a moment I thought they hadn't heard and I was going to shout again when suddenly our Maureen breaks away and comes up the road like an express train. The lad's standing still but only for a few seconds and then he's off in the opposite direction.

I was going to say to our Maureen that she owed us a favour but she came running up at a heck of a speed, straight at me, and past. And she seemed to be making the strangest sort of sounds. As if she was crying almost.

And she was. I should have recognised that sound. I'd heard her crying often enough. She was in the house and upstairs by the time I got in. Me mam's looking alarmed and she's got her arm round her, saying things like, "There now, there's nothing to worry about, pet," and patting her on the back. And me dad's standing up from his chair, the 'Journal' hanging from his hand.

"What's on now?" And he looks at me. "What you been up to?" he says.

It would be me to blame. I shook me head. I didn't know what any of this was about.

"What's up?" he said. "Come on, now."

I couldn't tell him. I didn't know. No good asking me.

And our Maureen's spluttering away, and me mam's saying, "There, there. Tell me all about it," and looking over Maureen's shoulder at me dad and nodding and winking at him to go into the scullery.

"Haway out, son," he says to me. He gets us by the arm and we go into the scullery leaving me mam and our Maureen. Me dad tried to find out from me what was wrong but I just said I didn't know.

A couple of minutes later, the door opened and me mam looked in.

"Come in, now," she said in a kind of whisper. "Nothing to get upset over."

And me dad and me went in.

"What's all this?" me dad said.

Me mam went over to him and whispered in his ear.

"Who you talkin' about?" he said.

"A lad called Barry," me mam said quietly. "Just take it easy. It's nothing."

"A lad? What's he been up to then?"

Me dad was suddenly very worried. I could see that. Me mam leaned forward again to whisper in his ear.

"He was going to do what?" he said. He was genuinely puzzled. Me mam wasn't a good whisperer, I suppose.

"He what?" he said.

Again, me mam whispered to him.

"A kiss?" me dad shouted. He looked horrified. "This lad's tried to kiss our Maureen?"

"Now don't get yourself upset," me mam said. "It's nothing to make a fuss about."

"Just as Ah said," me dad went on. "Didn't Ah warn ye? Ah knew what this would come to. And her just fourteen."

He went on talking to hisself. Nobody took any notice of him. You could hear me dad growling on. You heard words like, "... no daughter of mine ..." and "... disgraceful ..." and "... tan his backside if Ah catch'm ..."

As I say, nobody was bothering with what he said. Me mam was asking Maureen if she'd like a cup of tea or if she would just like to go off to bed and Maureen was putting on her Scarlett O'Hara look and probably enjoying all the fuss.

"And where was he?" me dad asked suddenly, jerking his thumb at me.

Well, our Maureen didn't go to the dancing class after that and I don't think she ever saw Barry again. But she went to the school dance and by all accounts really enjoyed it. Of course, me dad insisted on meeting her at the end. They argued about that for days beforehand but it was either that or she didn't go.

And, of course, I didn't have to escort her any more. But the football boots. I didn't like to mention them. And nobody else did.

Then one day me Auntie Louie called in as she always did once or twice every week. She had a bit talk with me mam and then she says to me, "Oh, by the way, Ah brought ye a little present."

Good old Auntie Louie. She was always giving us things.

"Pair of football boots," she said. "They're second-hand, mind."

I wouldn't have called the king me uncle that day. They were smashing. Mind, they looked awful like the ones I'd had me eye on.

And as me Auntie Louie gave them to us, I saw me mam give her a long, slow wink.

THE MACARONI DANCERS

Me dad came in and you could tell there was something up.

"Finishin' Friday," he said. "That's it."

It shouldn't've been a surprise to any of us. He'd been on short time for a couple of months, but when it happened we were really upset. For different reasons, of course.

First thing our Maureen said was, "Oh, does that mean I won't get a lacrosse stick for Christmas? Oh, you promised."

Me mam looked at her really annoyed. I thought she was going to smack her at first but she didn't. She just smiled; forced herself to, I suppose.

"You'll get your lacrosse stick, Maureen," was what she said. "Ah said ye would." She sounded very determined about it. She looked at me. "And you'll get what Ah promised you."

Roller skates.

"There's supposed to be a war on," me dad said. "How can they stop fellers workin'? How can they be short of materials?"

He looked really angry but he said nothing more just

then. He went into the kitchen. He used to change out of his work clothes there because it was always warm. When he came back he looked really in the dumps. But there was me mam, never giving up.

"Now," she says, "it's a month to Christmas. Ah've got a bit put away. We'll not go short."

She went to where me dad was sitting down, fiddling with his pipe.

"And we'll have to try and find a job for your dad." She patted him on the shoulder. "We'll try, won't we?" she said.

"Aye," he answered her. But he didn't look too hopeful.

"And Ah'll try and get one as well," she said. "Just for the time being."

Our Maureen said nowt. But you could guess what she was thinking. Fancy having that burden of shame to carry and her only fourteen years old. Oh, the disgrace of it. Her mam going out to work and her at the Convent School.

But me mam was smiling all round, trying to cheer us all up. Trust her.

At least Maurice Russell was good value. He cheered us up at school. By, he was daft. He was worth his weight in daftness.

"Hey," he says to me one dinner time. "Come here, lad."

I went over to him. It was a bitter cold day. There was ice and snow all over the school yard but we weren't allowed inside till quarter to two. Maurice was keeping out of the worst of the wind, standing just inside the lav door. You could scarcely see his face. He was wearing one of those leather helmets that fastened under the chin and he had the peak down over his eyes. It must've belonged to a grown-up at one time. His boots were hand-me-downs as well and he'd have to grow fast to grow into them because they were already falling apart on his feet. And, as usual, he was the picture of happiness.

"Here," he says. "Have a look at this." He pulled a magazine out from under his jersey.

"Ever seen owt like this?" he says.

Course I had. But I never saw anything in a magazine to get steamed up about. No lad in our town should ever have got worked up by a picture of a woman with no clothes on. We could see full-sized women without a stitch on every day of our lives. You just had to go down to the Town Hall and there they were all in a row. There was about half a dozen of them with nowt on except a little tea towel across their fronts. But their chests and their behinds and everything else was bare. And they were holding great heavy electric lamps above their heads. Then, in the middle of them sits old Queen Victoria with her crown on, looking ninety if she's a day, and pretending not to notice the lasses on each side.

So there was no excuse for anybody getting worked up about pictures in a book. And that's what I told Maurice. I said the ones at the Town Hall were better because there was so many of them, and because they were bigger and because you could walk right round them.

Poor Maurice. I thought he was going to cry he was so disappointed. I began to feel sorry for him but then I thought, why, he is ten, time he got used to disappointment. Anyway, he put the magazine back up his jumper and I don't think he bothered to show it to anybody else.

I never gave it another thought, but he had cheered us up a bit. But I was more cheered up when me dad came in that night. It was his last day and he looked really hangdog. But not me mam.

"Now," she says, business-like and cheerful, "don't look so miserable. Ah've got ye something. Job starts on Monday."

You should've seen his face. It lit up.

"Ye've got us a job?"

"Didn't Ah say Ah would?" me mam answered. She was a very determined woman.

"What is it?" He seemed quite excited. I think he'd've taken anything because he loved going to work.

"Ah'll tell ye later," she says.

"Ye can tell us now," he said.

"No." She stared him in the eye and then looked at me and our Maureen. "Ah'll tell ye later."

He swallowed hard.

"D'ye mean it's menial?"

He was sitting in his chair and he didn't know whether to be angry or pleased.

"It's honest, isn't it?" he asked her. But he knew it was and he needn't've asked.

But she told him anyway.

"It's not menial. And it is honest," she said. "The only thing is it's not permanent. But we can look for something else in the meantime."

But she wouldn't say what it was in front of us.

"And, by the way," she says very casually, "Ah've got meself a job as well."

And she didn't say what that was in front of me and Maureen either.

"Hey."

Maurice was in his usual place in the door to the lavs before school started on the Monday afternoon. It was freezing cold and he had his hands in his pockets and he was jogging up and down. He had his leather helmet on, as usual. You could see his bare skin through the holes in his jumper. He'd got his pants from his brother and they went below his knees.

"Hey, lad," he says and he tugs me sleeve. "Ah bet ye've never seen real live'uns wi' no clothes on."

He laughed out loud and jogged up and down faster and he rubbed his hands together.

"Ye haven't, have ye?" he shouts. "Gan on. Tell us. Ye haven't, have ye?"

I'd never really thought about it.

"Live?" I said.

"Why aye," he shouts. "Real live'uns wi' no clothes." He stopped suddenly and looked quickly behind him, left, then right. He lowered his voice and leaned forward and whispered. "Ah know where ye can see some."

He winked slowly and then got hold of us by the elbow and took us into a corner of the lavs.

"There's a place near the ferry landin'," he said. "There's women wi' no clothes on there." He nodded his head very carefully. "Live'uns."

I couldn't understand what he was getting at.

"They do things for sailors and dockers," he whispered. "They take their clothes off."

"What for?" I said. "What do they do?"

He backed away from us. Then he put his hands above his head. He bent his wrists and then started twisting them in circles. Then he waggled his hips and rolled his eyes. I laughed because he looked a bit daft doing that in his leather helmet.

He started to sing:

"Wah-Wah Waaah Waaah Waah
Wah-Wah Waaah-eee Waaah-eee Wah"

He gave a snarly kind of grin. Then out came the words:

"All the Girls in France
Do the Macaroni Dance.
Wah-Wah Waaah Waaah Waah
Wah-Wah Waaah-eee Waaah-eee Wah"

He put his hands down to his sides and stopped his shimmying. Suddenly he looked very serious as if he was afraid I hadn't enjoyed his performance.

"D'ye want to hear the rest?" he asked us.

"Aye."

A great grin spread across his face and he started up again:

"All the girls in France
Do the Macaroni Dance.
Singin' Nelly put ya belly
Next to mine."

By, I laughed when I heard that. And Maurice broke off singing because he was laughing as well.

"Ah've got some more words," he said at last and he sang them.

We laughed and laughed.

Then he sang the whole lot three or four times more, still twisting and waggling and rolling.

When he finished he gave another of his grins.

"They do it near the ferry. In a house."

This was all new to me.

"But what d'they do?" I asked him.

He looked over his shoulder again just to make sure we were alone.

"The Macaroni Dance, man." He came close to us. He was whispering so loud you could've heard him outside. "They do the Macaroni Dance for the dockers. And for sailors."

I didn't know why, I told him.

"For the money, man. They get paid to do these dances. They take their clothes off."

It seemed daft to me.

"D'ye want to see them?" he said.

"Doin' this dance?"

He shook his head.

"Why no. But we can gan and see the lasses who do it. We can watch them gannin' in. They do it in the dinner times and at nights. We can gan down on Saturday morning."

It seemed to be a good idea. I'd never seen Macaroni Dancers before. How could I? Even if I had, I wouldn't've known. I hadn't heard of them before.

"They take their clothes off, ye know," he reminded us. "They've got no clothes on when they do it."

I wondered if they did the Macaroni Dance in this

weather. They must feel very cold. Mebbes the dances they did were quicker than the one Maurice had shown us.

"Come'n see them on Saturday mornin', man," he said, "If we're there at eleven we'll see them gannin' in."

"Aye, right," I said.

Me dad didn't really like what he was doing. He wanted to get back to his trade.

"That's what Ah'm trained for and that's what Ah like doin'," he kept telling me mam.

But he never told us what his new work was. Me and our Maureen wanted him to tell us but he wouldn't say. He would shake his head and me mam would frown so we had to stop asking.

Other times he was more hopeful about the future. He kept saying he'd heard there might be work after Christmas and if there was he'd definitely be taken on again.

"One of the first," he used to say. "Ah'll be one of the first they call back, have no fear of that."

And me mam never complained about what she was doing.

"Ah'm enjoying the job," she used to say. And like me dad she never told me and Maureen where she was working. But one thing was obvious. The new job was taking it out of her because she was there morning and night. Me dad used to pick her up at ten o'clock every night and he'd bring her home on the tram. She was dead beat but she never once complained.

On the Saturday morning, me and Maurice took the tram down to the market. It was only a couple of minutes from the ferry. It was another icy day and you could scarcely keep your feet. We went down towards the river and he pushed us into an empty shop doorway.

"There's the place," he said out of the corner of his mouth. He swivelled his eyes across the road and nodded across at a three storied house with a bright red door and bright red window frames. And even though it was daylight, they had a bright red electric light shining in the passage. The house really stood out. It was the only place with a coat of paint.

"That's where they do it," Maurice told us. "In there."

Funny, I thought, you'd think if they wrote songs about it they'd do it in better places than that. Even though it was painted, it looked a bit old and run down.

"Here's the first'un," Maurice said and he gave us a thump with his elbow.

It wasn't hard to tell how he knew. She really stood out. She had a little hat on with a veil and a fur cape. Her dress was silky and she had high heels and even though the road was icy she never slipped but just walked along so daintily. She was covered in bright lipstick and face powder. She looked different from everybody else in the street that morning. She looked as near a film star as anything I'd ever seen. She was beautiful and she was smoking a cigarette and she looked really daring.

But she didn't go in the house. Mebbes Maurice had it wrong.

"No, man," he says very knowledgeably, "they have a drink or two in there first."

She was just disappearing into the 'Sir Robert Peel', just a door or two up from the house.

"That's where they meet," Maurice said. "Then if there's any sailors or dockers who want to see them dance, they take them next door."

I began to wonder if it was only sailors and dockers they did the Macaroni Dance for.

It was bitter cold in the doorway, that real nasty cold you get in December, but because it was becoming so interesting I scarcely noticed it. Some more Macaroni Dancers came along. I'd never seen so many beautiful girls. You could tell, even from where we were over the road, that they were very beautiful. There was a couple of tall ones, one very blonde and the other black haired and although they were so smart, they weren't too stuck up to speak to the fellers in the street. There was a little fat'un as well and she was very cheerful and kind looking. Another one had a shortish kind of dress and even in the dullness of the day the gold bracelet on her ankle twinkled away.

It cheered me up to see such colourful girls. And they all went into the 'Sir Robert Peel'.

After about ten minutes another couple came along. The tall one was the most beautiful girl I'd ever seen. She came out of your dreams. She was beyond description. She was tall and graceful. She walked as if she owned the pavement. She had this lovely smile on her face. She was talking to this other woman who wasn't as beautiful or tall but she did look very, very nice. She had a kind face and she was smart.......

... She was wearing her best frock ... carrying the handbag me dad had given her ... for her birthday...

Of course, Maurice didn't know her. If he had, I don't know what he'd've said. Daft lad. Probably something like, "Here, your mam's a Macaroni Dancer."

But I wouldn't have waited to listen. Because I didn't stop. I ran. I just ran and ran, never pausing, just ran. All the way.

And when I got home nobody was in. I looked in every room for me mam but I knew I wouldn't find her.

So I sat on the settee.

I wouldn't have liked anybody to see us cry. Not like that. Not as much as I did that day.

Later, I heard me dad running up the stairs. He was breathless when he came in. When I looked up I saw him with his hair flopping over his forehead, the sweat on his brow. He'd run up from the tram stop, he said. He was in a hurry. He had only an hour for his dinner.

He laughed.

"To think," he said, "Saturday afternoon. Ah should be goin' to the match. Ah should be settin' off now, by rights."

He tutted.

Then he looked at us closely.

"What's the matter with you?" he asked us.

I shook me head.

He turned the ends of his mouth down but he didn't say anything for a moment. Then, he said, "Has the postie been?"

I didn't know but before I could say anything, he spotted an envelope on the mantlepiece.

"Aye, he has," he said. "Your mam must've put it up there."

He took the envelope in his hand but he didn't open it straightaway. It was as if he was nervous of what was inside.

"Feller at work," he said. "Only temporary, like me. He had a letter this morning."

As if that explained it. He twisted the envelope round and read his name on the front.

"Ah've just dashed up. In case there's a one for me."

He put his finger inside the the flap and started to tear it.

"This feller, the letter he's had is to tell him there's a job in the New Year."

His fingers were trembling. He was putting off reading it. He hadn't even unfolded the sheet he'd taken out of the envelope. He kept looking at us and half smiling.

"They've got an order for a minesweeper," he said. "They're takin' some of the lads back on."

And it seemed to take him ages to open the sheet of paper out and even longer to read what was in it.

At last, he said in a very quiet voice, "Ah'm startin' on the third of January. Full time."

He didn't say any more. He stood and stroked his chin as if he was thinking hard and then he went through to the scullery for a bit. Then came back in to where I was.

"So," he said, and he was rubbing his hands together and looking really pleased with hisself, "full time, eh?"

He reached down and tapped us on the shoulder.

"Maureen'll get her lacrosse stick, eh?"

The idea tickled him and he started laughing.

"By lad," he said, shaking his head, "lacrosse, if ye please."

"Will me mam have to go on workin'?"

The smile left his face. He looked as if he hadn't thought of me mam. He took his pipe out and started filling it.

"Of course she won't go on workin'," he said at last. "No need anymore."

When he saw us crying, he was surprised. He didn't know what to say quite. Then he put his arm round us.

"What's the matter?"

At first I couldn't say anything. Then after a long time I told him why I was upset, told him about the Macaroni Dancers and the sailors and the dockers and the 'Sir Robert Peel' and everything.

And he seemed sad about it hisself.

"Don't worry," he said. "Ah don't like her workin' down there."

He took his hanky out and dried me eyes.

"It's not what ye think," he said after a while. "She's not a Macaroni Dancer." He stopped a minute. "Anyway, where'd ye get that name for them? Macaroni Dancers?"

I couldn't tell him about Maurice's song. It was too daft.

"No, son, she's only workin' behind the bar," he told us after we talked a bit.

So that was it.

"She was determined to get herself somethin'. We weren't goin' to have a rotten Christmas. She was determined about that." He smiled a moment. "Ye know your mam, what she's like."

And I did.

"But she didn't let on to you and Maureen. Really because Maureen'd be so upset, her mam workin' in a bar."

He sighed.

"Especially down there by the ferry. But that's all that was goin'," he said. "And she knew the manager."

"Are they all right, dad?" I asked him. "Those others? The Macaroni Dancers?" I couldn't forget I'd seen me mam with one of them. And they'd looked so nice and beautiful.

"Salt of the earth," he said. "No need to worry about them. Your mam gets on with them champion."

And he told us about what mattered was working hard at honest work and doing the best you could.

"Don't worry if it's menial," he said. "As long as ye do your best at honest work."

It didn't take him long to decide to take us back to work with him.

"Ye'd better come and see us. It's not like the shipyard, ye know," he told us on the tram. "It's not a trade but it's all right. For the time bein'."

So he took us back to Binns. Me dad, a craftsman, working in a shop. You couldn't have believed it.

But I watched him all afternoon and he was good at it. He worked hard and in a way there was a lot of skill in it, the way he did it.

The bairns sat on his knee. Some of them pulled at his cotton wool beard. Some of them tried to tug the red hood over his eyes. Some of them were in tears when they first came to him but he talked to them ever so gently and they were soon right as rain. They all went out with their mams and dads and they were smiling and clutching their Christmas presents.

He was good at it, me dad. No need for him to be ashamed of what he was doing. No need for me mam either. And no need for me and our Maureen to be ashamed of them.

Mebbes there was no need even for the Macaroni Dancers to be ashamed of themselves either. I hoped not.